A Change of Plans

A short story spin off from Dancing Around the Cop (book 2 of the Alpha and Omega series)

By Lisa Oliver

A Change of Plans (Alpha and Omega # 6)

Copyright © Lisa Oliver, 2017

ALL RIGHTS RESERVED

Cover Design by Lisa Oliver

Cover Model –courtesy of Paul Henry Serres Photography. License ABA_237

Background – Dreamstime.com

First Edition May 2017

Table of Contents

Dedication

My readers are always such a constant joy to me – the way you reach out through social media, sharing pictures and wonderful stories. Please believe me when I say this book could not have been written without you. Your support means more than you could ever know, so thank you.

And there are those wonderful people behind the scenes who do so much to help keep me on track and get the word out about my books. Phil, Judy, Mary, Torhild, Leah, my wonderful PA Avril, and all my lovely friends in Lisa's Wolfpack. You bring sunshine into my life.

Thank you.

Chapter One

"Fucking hell, that's Richard's brother?" Sully whistled under his breath as he and Zander watched Richard greeting a muscle-mountain with closely cropped blond hair. The airport was crowded but Richard was as tall as him and Zander, standing out from the rest. The brother's head rose a few inches higher; his harsh military haircut and squared shoulders screamed Marine.

"He'd snap you like a twig," Zander chuckled. "I thought you were looking for someone smaller to scratch an itch. I'm sure Terry's friend Charlie would be interested if you smiled in his direction."

"He's looking for a relationship," Sully muttered, watching as Richard and his brother came closer. "I wouldn't be good for him with my hours. Besides, he's built like Terry; it'd be me snapping him in half."

"Don't mess with a marine," Zander warned as he plastered a professional smile on his face and stepped forward. "Gunnery Sergeant Thorne? A pleasure to meet you. I'm Detective Zander Samuels." He held out his hand and the bigger man took it. Sully could pick up a weird vibe coming from the two men; the handshake taking longer than necessary. *Damn it. Just my luck the marine prefers brunettes, although Terry won't be pleased.*

"You can call me Q." The marine said roughly giving Zander's hand a final squeeze before dropping it.

"And this is Sully Roberts," Richard said, with an edge to his voice. "He's a detective too. He and Zander used to work together, but he's currently assigned to the SWAT team."

No need to remind me, asshole, Sully's smile was forced as he held out his hand to the marine who seemed reluctant to take it. Feeling decidedly snubbed, Sully went to drop his, but at the last-minute Q took it, the work-hardened fingers sending a tingle of electricity through his arm. *My gods, I want this man;* Sully's eyes widened at the thought and he hurriedly dropped Q's hand. "I'll go get the car. Were you coming out with us...er...Q, or shall we drop you somewhere first?"

"Oh, I'm coming," Q's eyes were darker than Richard's brilliant blue ones but they looked as though they could see into his very soul. "I'm definitely coming along."

"Yeah...er...right...I'll just go...." Sully's usual confidence deserted him and he fled the airport terminal, eager for some fresh air. There was a definite bite in the air although Sully knew his cheeks were still heated when he reached the car. Checking he was alone, he quickly thumped his cock. "Looking is one thing," he muttered to the lump in his pants, "but don't go getting any ideas."

Yes, Q was a magnificent muscle-bound hunk, but Sully knew the chances of both brothers being gay were slim to none, especially with Q being a marine. Sully worked out at the gym every day and his job kept him in peak condition, but Zander was right, Q could crush him like a bug. *But oh, what a way to go,* he thought shaking his head as he got into the car. *What a way to go.*

/~/~/~/~/

"What the hell are you doing?" Richard hissed at his brother as they waited for Sully to collect the car. "First you try to crush Zander's hand to dust and then you're looking at Sully like you want to eat him. He's barely out of the closet."

"Mate," Q said bluntly his eyes scanning the exits and everyone milling around. "Mine," he added for emphasis. "And Zander's hand is fine."

"You mean you and Sully?" Zander bent over, laughing like a loon, his crushed hand apparently forgotten.

Damn it, Richard should've warned me he was bringing another shifter along. Q refused to feel sorry for trying to establish his dominance in a human way. But Zander's reaction to what was a life-changing decision annoyed him.

"You have one, I can smell him. An omega, if I'm not mistaken."

"Don't you touch my m...Terry," Zander amended quickly although no one was paying attention to them. The joys of being in an airport; everyone always had somewhere else to be.

"We don't fight among ourselves, Q," Richard warned quietly. "We're all loners here and have learned to get along. Hold your temper. Zander's Terry is very good friends with the man I'm seeing and neither one of them deserves any grief from you."

Q bit his tongue. Seeing Richard friendly with another Alpha who wasn't pack or mate was his first shock of the evening. Meeting a human mate was the second. Now Q's wolf, who put up with a lot during his time in the Marines was edgy and anxious. It was night; danger lurked around every corner and their mate was out there alone.

"Sully's a detective," Zander said, watching the crowds and doing some fidgeting of his own. "He knows how to handle himself."

"Does Sully know about us?"

"In a way. He just recently learned about it, but he thinks it's only me and Terry. He doesn't know about Richard."

Damn, that would've made things a lot easier. But fuck, what am I thinking? I can't take a mate. Especially not male. What about my team, my work? I won't be able to re-enlist. Q thought back to the conversation he'd had with his lieutenant the previous day. He was due for re-enlistment; his second four-year term coming to an end in another month. His CO indicated promotion would be available to him if he chose to sign up for another four years, but something at the time held Q back. That was why he was on a month's leave; to think about his future at his CO's suggestion.

Was it only this morning I thought I didn't have anything to mull over? He had a good platoon, decent sergeants under him and while his wolf pined for the touch of others, the action they'd seen and the comradeship made up for a lot over eight years. He knew they'd be deployed soon and he planned on going. But now…Q looked up to see Richard watching him anxiously.

"I'll go slow," he promised, unsure how he'd keep that promise but vowing he would. "I'm on a month's leave."

Richard looked as if he wanted to say more; Q knew since his brother-in-law died, Richard was all for mates, mating and spending as much time with mates as possible. But a car pulled up, Sully at the wheel and Q's lust rendered him speechless; clearly whatever Richard was going to say wasn't suitable for human ears. He threw his bag in the trunk and squeezed his frame into the seat behind Sully. In the confines of the car, Sully's scent, a sweet mix of citrus and brandy singed his nostrils and he hid his claws under his legs. *It's going to be a freaking long evening.*

Chapter Two

He's looking at me again. Sully surreptitiously wiped across his chin, worried he might have food stuck to it. Dinner was lovely, or at least he assumed it was. Sully ate on autopilot. He could feel Q's eyes on him, but every time he looked up the man seemed to be watching the crowds. His cock was screaming at him to make a move; his head and guts were warning him that was a bad idea.

"Your phone's ringing," Charlie smiled as he poked Sully in the ribs. Charlie was the only one of Terry's friends still single; well, apart from Q who looked big enough to terrify anyone and Sully didn't mind chatting to him, even if he had no plans of taking anything any further. Small, like all of Terry's friends, Charlie's hopeful look bordered on desperate a couple of times throughout the meal; something Sully tried to ignore.

"Thanks." Sully didn't offer any explanation of why he hadn't heard his phone. What could he say? *I can't tell if the man across from me wants to lick me all over or throttle me and it's bugging me?* Yeah. That wouldn't go over well. He slid from the booth, answering his phone as he went, heading outside where things were a lot quieter.

"Detective Roberts, what's up?" He asked, recognizing the number as the dispatch office.

"Detective Roberts, we have a domestic situation; firearms on the scene. Backup has been requested by local officers," the calm voice sounded as though she was talking about the weather, but Sully's adrenalin surged. "Please proceed to the address I will text you and report to Commander Latham."

"Shit," Sully looked down at his jeans and shirt. "Affirmative, Dispatch. Will be there in fifteen minutes."

The dispatch officer clicked off without comment and Sully hurried inside. He was going to need to borrow Zander's car; the keys were still snug in his pocket. Conscious of Q following his every move, he pulled Zander aside and quickly explained the situation. Zander looked torn, as though wanting to come along, but they didn't work together anymore and with a slap on his shoulder and a "keep your head down" Zander went back to his friends and Sully ran back to the car. Gunning the motor as he sped past the club, he swore he saw Q standing at the door; ignoring what could only be a flight of fancy, Sully focused on the road and the evening ahead. Richard's brother wasn't going to distract him, at least until the domestic situation was resolved.

/~/~/~/~/

"Q, for the love of all that's holy, what's got into you?" Q wasn't used to being manhandled into a bathroom, especially in a club, but he could see Richard was pissed and went quietly. Maybe charging out of the club after a work-focused mate was a bit much. But he wasn't backing down to his brother.

"My mate just went storming off. That damned smug friend of yours simply says 'work', like it's none of my concern. How did you expect me to react?"

"By tipping over the table; upsetting Terry and his friends? Nearly getting us thrown out?"

"Upsetting your little drama queen, you mean. He yelled because he smudged his mascara and got a mayonnaise stain on his jeans. I said I'd pay for dry-cleaning." Q paced, five steps one way, five steps back. His fangs had dropped, his claws digging into his palms. He was in danger of losing his shit; his wolf had never been as pushy before. *You've never met a mate before.*

"One," Richard got right in his face. "Never insult Roy again. He might not be your type, but he's fun and my wolf likes him and wants to protect him."

Q bit back his response. He'd been the one picking up the pieces when Richard's mate died in a tragic accident. The man was shattered and Q worried for months he'd have to bury his brother. It had been a long road back for Richard and Q wouldn't demean his brother's choices now.

"Two," Richard wasn't finished. "Sully might be yours, but he's not wearing your mark; you've barely spoken two words to him and he has a job to do. You're a marine; you understand loyalty, honor and following orders."

Yes, Q did; hence his conflict. He wanted Sully; every cell in his body wanted to claim the man. But if he did...it seems Richard was following a similar thought.

"How you gonna claim the man, Q? You get sent all over the world. Hell, it can be months before I hear from you. You can't stash Sully in base housing and then disappear for goodness knows how long."

"He could stay here; do his job. I can come back when I'm on leave," but even as the words tumbled out of Q's mouth, he knew he was lying to himself. Richard knew it too.

"And your animal half is going to accept you being on different continents; him in dangerous situations every day, knowing you are too? You'll go mad without him."

"What am I meant to do?" Q spat out. "His scent is clogging my nostrils; all I can see in my head is his ass when he walked out. My wolf is this close," he held up his hand, thumb and forefinger millimeters apart, claws fully extended, "to tracking him down."

"First, you breathe," Richard said, his hands a solid weight on Q's shoulders. "In and out, with me, just breathe." Q dutifully inhaled and exhaled, following the rise and fall of Richard's chest. "That's better," Richard said as Q's claws receded. "Now," he said gently, "We need to get back to my place. I already told Roy I'll see him for lunch tomorrow. He knows you've just got into town and totally understands the situation. Then we can talk; really talk and see if we can't work out a solution that will work for you and Sully."

Q followed, even though his inner self wasn't happy about it. "How did you meet Zander, anyway?" He asked as he passed their now empty table. Clearly, his temper had caused a swift end to the night.

"I was dating Terry, just to piss him off, although we'd seen each other around for years before that little incident," Richard laughed as he raised his hand for a taxi. "Oh, and here's another delicious tidbit, if you're interested. When Sully first saw Zander furry, he pointed a gun at him."

"Couldn't have happened to a nicer guy," Q chuckled as he bent to get into the taxi. "But hey, how will I know Sully's all right? We should go and check on him, right? You know where he lives?" He shuffled over so Richard could get in beside him.

"Zander has my number. I think he plans on speaking to Sully in the morning, so if you don't want 'this', you'd better let me know now. Zander thinks a lot of his friend and will be pissed if you go running out of town leaving Sully on his own after he's laid the groundwork for you."

"Of course, I want 'this'," Q mimicked Richard's air quotes. "I just…." Q trailed off, conscious of the driver listening in on every word. *Improvise. Adapt. Overcome.* The Marine's motto went around and around in his head. Q knew how to do it; he'd been trained to do it. But when the improvising and adapting meant leaving his life of eight years...he didn't think that was what the Marines had in mind.

Chapter Three

"Hey, Zander, I wasn't expecting to see you so bright and early. Did Terry kick you out of bed?" Sully stood back hanging onto his towel as he let his longtime friend into the house. "I just got out of the shower. Go and help yourself to coffee and I'll put some pants on."

"I wanted to catch you before you went to the gym," Zander called out as he made his way to the kitchen and Sully ducked into the bedroom.

His house was a small, one-story ranch style with just two bedrooms and two bathrooms. Personally, he preferred Zander's house; especially since Terry added touches of color and warmth to Zander's previously austere home. Zander's had a warm and comfortable feel and Sully shook his head as he took in his spartan room. *Maybe I should ask Terry for some advice on soft furnishings.*

Yanking on a pair of sweats, wondering where his sudden burst of domesticity came from, Sully went back out into the kitchen. "So, what's up? It takes a lot to get you out of bed this time of the morning since Terry's keeping it warm for you. Surely, you're not here to make sure I got back from the job last night."

"I'll thank you not to mention Terry and bed in the same sentence," Zander showed his teeth and Sully laughed. "Actually, I am here to check on you, which I've done. But I also had a question. What did you think of Q?"

"Richard's brother? What is this, high school?" Sully was stalling. Seemed he couldn't do anything but think of the man. It was one of the reasons he needed another shower. "He's very intense. Handsome if you like that sort of thing. But hey, I behaved myself. I didn't go rubbing off on his leg or anything. I'm not that hard-up."

Zander looked down at his mug and Sully felt a frisson of unease running down his spine. "I didn't do anything, did I? Look, I didn't sit next to him; I talked to Charlie most of the night. Oh, gods, he doesn't think I've got the hots for him, does he? What the hell did I do?" The last thing Sully needed was an angry Marine breathing down his neck. He'd got enough grief from Latham the night before for being distracted.

Zander took a sip of his coffee, looked up at the ceiling and then back at Sully. "You remember my wolf."

Sully nodded. It's not like it was something he'd forget. Seeing his best friend turn into a furry four-legged animal didn't happen every day. He was still embarrassed he'd pulled a gun on his friend; the reason he was still on the SWAT team.

"And you know Terry's one too."

"Yeah, you explained you guys were mates, although I haven't seen Terry furry. I bet he's cute."

Zander chuckled. "Don't let him hear you call him that. But yeah, okay, what I haven't told you before because it wasn't my secret to tell is that Richard and Q are wolf shifters too."

"Q and Richard?" Q, Sully could understand. The guy reeked of animal magnetism; Sully could easily imagine him turning into a man-eating animal. But Richard? Sully shrugged. A wolf in a suit. Who knew? But then he had a horrible thought and busied himself looking for a mug, his cheeks flaming. "They could smell me, couldn't they? How aroused I was when I met Q. Oh my god, I am so sorry, but how the hell was I supposed to know? Look, this must happen to you guys all the time. Don't tell me Q's gunning for me now. It was a perfectly honest reaction; I didn't do anything about it."

"Q's gunning for you all right," Zander sniggered, "but not in the way you're thinking. You know about me and Terry, right? I explained about mates."

"Yeah," Sully said slowly, still facing the cupboards. *He's not going to say, he's not going to say….*

"You're Q's mate."

He just had to go and say it. "I wouldn't have thought this was a newsflash to anyone; but I'm human, not an omega wolf," Sully said, busy doctoring his coffee. "I know my parents; I'm not adopted and there's no way in hell, I run around on four legs. Q must have his wires crossed, or he's taken one too many hits on the nose."

"Shifters can have non-shifter mates, or other shifters, or anyone really. Believe me, we alpha wolf shifters know when we scent a mate. He's not mistaken. You should've seen him after you left. He went ballistic and damn near got us kicked out."

"So tell me, that attitude right there; just from me having to go to work. How on earth is a 'mating' between us going to work?" Sully slammed his coffee mug on the countertop and turned, facing his seemingly unconcerned friend. "You warned me off him last night, and believe me, I know better than to mess with a man bigger than me. He didn't even talk to me so I'm still thinking he's got his wires crossed. But let's say you're right; let's assume I am his mate. What about our jobs? He doesn't have a job; he has a career, just like I do. I thought you shifters couldn't bear to be without your mates? Hell, you're always slinking off to find Terry at lunchtime and you go home faithfully every freaking night. I get called out at night and it wouldn't make any difference anyway because my so-called mate would be overseas getting shot at and bombs thrown at him."

"I didn't say it would be easy," Zander said. Sully wanted to slap that unruffled look right off the handsome man's face. "Q apparently didn't say anything last night because he wasn't sure what he was going to do."

"Oh great," Sully grabbed a cloth and started wiping up the coffee he spilled. "Well, thanks for telling me, although I don't know why you bothered. Believe it or not, humans have feelings too and I don't take kindly to being rejected before the damned man even gets to know me. But fine. Thanks for the warning; I'll stay out of your guy's way until his leave is up. Can't upset the precious wolf shifter, now can I? I mean, good heaven's, what would happen if he lost control and accidentally bit me? Not that a Marine would ever lose control. Now, piss off, will you? I've got to go to the gym and I'm sure you've got work to do."

"I gave him your number. He ain't giving up on you," Zander grinned as he put his coffee cup on the counter. "My advice?" He whispered in Sully's ear. "Invest in a butt plug if you don't have one already. Make it a big one. Have a great day." He sauntered off laughing and Sully heard the front door slam.

"Fucking bastard," Sully muttered as he threw the cups into the sink, scouring them angrily under the tap. "Comes in here, drops a bombshell like that and then wanders off to his happy life laughing his fool head off. Butt plug indeed. What makes him think...?" Sully's eyes widened and he dropped the mug and scurried into the bedroom, scanning the room. There was nothing out of place. His bed needed straightening, but there was nothing incriminating anyone could see. Going over to his dresser, he crouched and opened the lower drawer. His toys were all there.

"Zander doesn't know about this," he mused, hefting one of his dildos and slapping it in his other hand, "so why did he...?" His eyes widening, Sully looked at the lump of silicone in his hand. "Bigger than that?" He wondered, holding it up. He gulped and then put the dildo back where he got it from, slamming the drawer shut.

"Go to the gym. Focus on my day. Don't go daydreaming about some huge marine slamming into my ass." Yep, that sort of thinking wasn't going to make Sully's workout any easier.

Chapter Four

"I need to know how Ian died," Q said bluntly as Richard shuffled into the kitchen, still looking half-asleep. Having been up since 0500 hours and completed his run and his morning exercise routine; Q was showered and dressed, ready for his next mission: claiming his mate. But before he did, he wanted to be absolutely sure he was doing the right thing.

"Fuck, you know how to hit someone with a sledgehammer before they're even awake," Richard complained, heading straight for the coffee pot. "Why do we need to rehash this old stuff anyway? Ian's been dead ten years. Yes, I still miss him, but I'm moving on. I'm with Roy now and I think if things continue working out, I'm going to tell him about me."

"I'm pleased for you," and Q was. Sure, Richard would never have a true mate like Ian again, but he could bond with this Roy, which would stop the human from aging. Roy would heal faster; his reflexes would speed up and he'd be a lot stronger too. That's why Q didn't understand how come Ian died. It wasn't the sort of question he could ask when Richard was ready to kill himself. In the months that followed, Q hadn't liked to bring it up and over time it became a moot point. But now Q was desperate to know. "I'm worried about claiming Sully. I'm not sure I'd cope like you did if he dies on me. He's in a dangerous job."

Richard sighed and came over to the table, sitting opposite Q. He took a long sip of his coffee before answering. "I thought you'd made up your mind last night. But fine, if you have to know, Ian was decapitated," he said quietly. "It was a freak motorcycle accident. It was a wet night but Ian was a good rider, which is why I didn't fret when he said he needed to go out for cigarettes. He'd done it a hundred times before. But that night his wheel slipped on a patch of oil on the road; his bike went into a skid and his head was torn off by the wheel of an oncoming truck. That poor driver never got behind the wheel again."

"Fuck, I'm sorry." Q knew it was bad; knew it had to be something severe to kill a mate. But he'd never imagined something so graphic. Swallowing hard, he asked, "A shot though. Is it possible a shot could kill Sully? He's on the SWAT team; that means shooting and him being in the line of fire."

Putting his mug on the table, Richard reached over, grabbing one of Q's hands. "I'm going to tell you, much the same as I told Zander when he was being an ass about his mate. You only get one. We only get one person in our hellishly long existence to call our true mate. If someone told me, when I met Ian, that he was going to die after less than twenty years together, I'd have still claimed him. Those years were the happiest of my life and his death can't take away those memories. They'll always be with me. And yes, it's taken me a long time, but I'm finally ready to open my heart again. I know it won't be the same thing; a bond with Roy will never have the same intensity as the love I shared with Ian. But I love Roy and care for him and I'll protect him as much as I'm able. You can't fear death, Q. Surely, you of all people should know that."

"I see so much of it," Q whispered as he stared down at their joined hands. "Every time we go away, that's all I see. The smell, fuck it gets to me; the despair, the anger, and the hatred. Even from the people we're trying to help. God, it scars my soul. But that's what I'm trained for. Keep going, follow orders and leave no man behind."

"How long have you been fighting?" Richard asked. "I know you went into the Marines after Ian's death, but fuck, how many armies have you been in?"

Q thought for a moment. "Seven, I think," he replied. "I enlisted for the first time when I was eighteen."

"The best part of fifty years, in other words," Richard shook his head, his smile kind. "Don't you think it's about time you did something else? Do you know I can't remember the last time I heard you laugh, really laugh. You're always so guarded and careful. Your wolf must go through hell, not being able to shift for months at a time."

"He's gotten used to it," Q said, although he knew what his brother was saying was true. Living around humans 24/7, Q watched every word, every action, making sure he never gave himself away. Alpha born, he forced his wolf back and followed orders, even when he didn't agree with them. Q hadn't realized how tired he was; how exhausting it had been, hiding his true nature. "Sully's got a career too; you saw how quickly he disappeared last night. He's not going to just quit his job and live on a ranch with me somewhere."

"A ranch? Really?" Richard quirked his brow. "Maybe not, but then I don't know Sully very well. Until a month ago, he was so far in the closet he was living in Narnia. Family issues, Zander tells me; but if he has you, and he needs to escape his family, then a ranch in the middle of nowhere might just be the ticket."

"I can't see him giving up his job." Q had been up half the night worrying about that very thing. The other half had been worrying about how his men would react to the news, but Richard couldn't help with that.

"One thing meeting Ian taught me was, once claimed, the mating pull works just as strongly both ways even if our mate is human." Richard smiled. "I was just starting out in law when I met Ian; working punishingly long hours. I tried to get home as early as I could, but I was putting in sixteen-hour days. Poor Ian was working in a factory. He was up at dawn and home by five. He gave that up within a week and do you know why?"

"You told him you could support him?" Q couldn't see any factory worker sticking it out in a menial job unless they had to.

"It had nothing to do with money. It was because Ian wanted to be with me. He'd come in every lunch hour and then again about five when the head honchos went home. He'd bring me food and we'd slip away." Shaking his head, Richard laughed. "I'm sure for those first two years we spent most of our mated life in supply closets. I told him time and time again he didn't have to. But every night, without fail, the two of us would be in my little cubicle. He'd read me cases I needed for my work, points of law, obscure bits of information he'd find in exhaustive searches. I swear by the time those two years were up and I got my first partnership, he knew more about the law than I did."

Q felt the edges of his lips twitch at the happiness in his brother's voice. "Do you think Roy will be like that?"

"No, but my circumstances have changed too. Roy designs lighting for shows in town. I work for myself and have staff. I'm the one visiting him and that makes him feel special. I've been dying to tell him about my wolf, but Terry and Zander said to wait just a little while longer. They're going to help me. Terry's sure Roy's going to be pissed off he hasn't been allowed into the secret before now."

"Sounds like you've got a feisty one on your hands. Are you sure you want to bond with him?"

Richard nodded and then stood up. "As a Marine, I guess you have a plan to win Sully's heart?"

"I was thinking dinner and a club?"

"Sports teams, bro, think sports teams. Zander said Sully is a huge fan of anything sporty. There's a game tonight and I happen to have two tickets."

"Won't Roy want to go?"

Snorting, Richard then laughed out loud. "Nope. I mentioned it and got 'the look.' We're going to see the Divas over at the revamped Club Blue. That's more his style."

"I'll take the tickets." Q would have preferred a more intimate evening, but if Sully was into sports, then it was his job to make his mate happy. Hopefully, Sully wasn't one of those frenzied fans with the big foam hands and noise makers. Although, on reflection, it might be better if he was. Then Q wouldn't have the urge to jump him every five minutes.

Chapter Five

Sully slammed his work locker shut and found himself face to face with Gibson. "What's up Gib? Finished for the day?"

"Yeah," Gibson looked around the locker room; a couple of the team members were watching and a prickle ran up Sully's spine. "Wondered if you wanted to come and have a few beers with us. Heard you were quite the lady's man when you were in vice; thought you could give us lonely hearts a few pointers."

"Ancient history," Sully forced himself to chuckle. His spidey senses were screaming he was in trouble and he wasn't the type to ignore them. "Sorry, can't tonight. I'm meeting a friend. Maybe some other time."

"This friend one of those fags you've been seen hanging around with?" There was a nasty tone in Gibson's voice and Sully forced his feet to remain where they were.

"Who I associate with outside of working hours is my business." He kept his voice as steady as possible while his insides were screaming for him to run or throw a punch. "But for your information, my 'date' for the evening is a marine. Brother of a friend of mine. I'm showing him around town while he's on leave. Got a problem with that?"

Gibson stepped back. "Nah, all good. Totally respect a man in uniform."

Just not mine, Scully thought as he sauntered out of the locker room; he was rattled. *They know. Fuck, they know. And now I have a mate. Fuck, I wish I was still partners with Zander. Damn, I've been a fucking fool.*

At least your mate's a marine, the devil on his shoulder piped up. *He can handle himself.*

Sully knew that was true, and it wasn't as though he lied to his teammates. But clearly, someone had seen him out with Zander and his friends. Gibson was trying to cause trouble and from the vibe in the locker room, it seemed he had backup. *And unless I find a way to sort out this situation, I won't have.*

Worrying his bottom lip, Sully hurried to his car. He was happy and worried, nervous and scared and none of that was helping his stomach. Q was an alpha wolf shifter. They were mates, or at least that's what Q politely explained when he called and asked him on a date. And this was a date; Q was firm about that too. A real date. His first date with a man. *Fuck, I just know I'm going to do something stupid.*

/~/~/~/~/

Q parked his rental in front of the address he'd been given, quickly scanning the area. The neighborhood was good; house small; no obvious concerns, but it was hard for him to shake the habits of a lifetime. His hand was on the door handle when

Sully came out of his house. As he turned to lock his front door, Q was afforded a beautiful view of what could only be described as a fuckable ass. *Oh damn, this is going to be a long evening. Smile. Richard said to smile.* He was sure his cheeks creaked as he tried it.

"Everything, okay?" Sully asked as he slid into the passenger seat, his scent hitting Q's nose like a bomb. "You looked worried about something."

"I was trying to smile," Q said, giving up the attempt and started the car. "Richard said it would make me look more approachable."

Sully's smile came easily. "Honest. That's a good start and if you don't mind me saying so, you've got nothing to worry about in the looks department."

Oh gods, is my wolf dancing? What the hell? Q grunted his thanks and got the car moving. He had a sneaky suspicion he was meant to say something positive about Sully's looks in return. Unfortunately, the only compliments he'd given in fifty years were of the "good job soldier" variety. "Did you have problems on your job last night?"

"Nothing I haven't faced before," Sully said, watching out his side window. "The man was high on something, waving his rifle around. He held a woman and two children hostage. When he wouldn't stand down, he was clipped on the arm, fell to the ground and the woman started screaming at us because he was hurt. Children crying, not sure what's going on." Sully's sigh was long and heartfelt. "I hate it when that happens."

"I know the feeling," Q said. "But you're part of a good team, right?" Comradeship was something that always helped lessen the impact of a negative situation. It didn't take it away, or minimize the horrors of what was seen, but sometimes, just knowing someone else was going through the same thing did help.

"Depends on your definition of a team," Sully said. "For a long time, it was just me and Zander; we worked as partners on the vice squad. Then…I stuffed up. There's no other way to say it and now I'm with a group of guys already stirring shit because I've been seen out with Zander and Terry."

Frowning, Q risked a quick look at his mate. "Being gay's not a crime, especially among shifters."

"Maybe, maybe not, but don't you get strange looks when you go out with guys?"

"I guess we'll find out." Q parked two shops down from the restaurant his brother assured him Sully would like.

"Wait," Sully said, and Q looked down to see his hand on his arm. Seeing him watching, Sully immediately removed it and he'd have grabbed it back except for the confusion on

Sully's face. "You're not gay? Then why are you doing this? Going out with me?"

"I thought Zander explained." It was Q's turn to be confused. "We're mates."

"Yeah, I get that. Apparently, your furry half thinks I smell great. But if you're not into men...I don't see how this could happen."

Q looked across at the restaurant; it looked fairly crowded. The game wouldn't be any better. "Do you want to get a burger and we'll drive somewhere? We need to talk."

"Sure, drive around the corner and about three blocks down is a food truck. They're good." Sully leaned back in his seat and Q started the car again. Sure enough, the truck was where Sully had indicated, the smells of cooking food had Q's mouth watering. He tapped his fingers on the small counter, waiting for their order to be cooked and served, his eyes flashing to Sully in the car every ten seconds. *How much has Zander told him about wolf shifters? I thought this mating was a slam dunk. Improvise and adapt – the burgers and a change of plans. Overcome – shit, I'm going to have to have the "talk".* Because Q knew, as he paid for and accepted the burgers, which smelled amazing, he couldn't claim his mate, until Sully understood what it meant to be with a wolf shifter.

Chapter Six

I knew it. Damn Gibson making me question shit. I knew I'd fucking screw things up. Now he doesn't want to be seen with me. Why did I open my big mouth? Sully watched as Q stalked, that was the only word that came to mind, Q stalked back to the car. *At least he plans on feeding me.*

He was conflicted; he knew he was and he also knew there was a good chance Q would scent some change in him, but since he'd got Q's call at lunchtime, Sully'd fluctuated between anticipation and panic. Zander had told him, ages ago, when he'd finally found his balls and apologized for filing the complaint, that Terry was everything to him. Sully had been honest at the time; he wanted what Zander had with Terry. That commitment, that sense of knowing no matter what life throws at you, you've always got someone watching your back.

And now it turns out he's not even gay and what am I? A freaking closet case. So much for anticipation. I should've saved myself the angst and gone out with the team instead. Sully slumped in his seat, barely noticing when Q got back in, handed over the bags of food and started the car.

"Where too?"

"Anywhere. I don't freaking care."

Q's lips tightened but he put the car in gear, Sully cursing himself in his head all the while. He was a grown man. A detective. He'd been trying to get his father to understand he was gay for years. Q was meant for him and damn, Sully couldn't ask for a better partner. One look at Q would shut his father up for good. But Sully didn't want to hide behind his mate's starched pants and military bearing.

"I'm gay." The words sounded loud against the uncomfortable silence of the car, but Sully felt better for saying it.

"Good." Q flicked him a quick glance but then focused on the road. Sully found himself fascinated by Q's grip on the steering wheel. Q had such big hands; squared off nails, thick fingers. Sully's ass muscles clenched.

"If we stay here," he said, forcing his eyes to the front of the car, "You're going to hear a lot of stories about me and women. They're all true."

Did Q just growl? Sully was sure he did. "I've never been in a relationship that's lasted longer than a month and that was only once; but it never stopped me getting laid at least once a week." Poor Susie, she was a lovely girl. The growls got louder and out of the corner of his eye, Sully noticed Q's knuckles were white. He had to say something fast. "When Zander told me about him and Terry and how they were mates, I really wanted one too. I'm glad it's you." *There, I didn't sound like too much of an idiot, did I?* Although from the silence, Sully guessed maybe he did.

/~/~/~/~/

Torture; Q thought he understood the meaning of the word. Being helpless, suffering and unable to do anything about it. Sully might not be inflicting physical wounds, but his outpouring of honesty, while Q was driving, combined with his scent which had Q's body hot enough to combust was driving him to distraction. It took every bit of his legendary control not to just pull over and rip the man's pants off. Spotting some trees and bushes, he quickly cut across two lanes and parked.

"We're walking," he said bluntly. "Bring the food."

Sully stepped out of the car, his boots crunching on the gravel as he followed Q across the sidewalk, over the small fence, and onto the grass. Q headed straight for a patch of shrubbery, set on the edge of the greenery. The park was almost empty; a lone jogger ran past, not even giving them a second look, but the play area was unoccupied; most people already at home settling into their evening routines. It wasn't late enough for the drug addicts and drunks to be roaming around. Q intended to be in a bed with Sully before it got that late.

"Put the food down here," he ordered, pointing to a patch on the ground. Surrounded by thicket, no one around, Q gave into his impulses, tugging Sully towards his chest and feasting on his mouth. A wiggle, a moan, and Sully's mouth opened, their bodies hard against each other; Sully's fingers leaving gouge marks on Q's back. His wolf howled his pleasure.

Sully's taste was everything Q dreamed of; warm aroused male. His lips were soft and full, the edge of day-old scruff abrasive on his cheek. His hair wasn't long enough for Q to get a tight hold, but Q cupped his head one-handed, refusing to let his mate go. Only when his head swam, his lungs screaming for air, did he pull back reluctantly.

"Rule one," he growled, "We don't ever speak of past partners."

"But I just wanted you…." Q kissed him again. His cock was full and heavy against his zipper and he ran his free hand down Sully's back, forcing their bodies even closer. Oh yeah, there may have been a hump or two.

"Rule two," he panted when his lungs insisted on working again, "No one else but me, man or woman, ever again. Understood?"

"Yes, but I…." Q heard yes, that's all he wanted to hear. Bending his head, he took Sully's lips softer this time and was rewarded with a whimper and a tentative tongue that quickly became voracious. Sully's mouth was made for him; his body honed and strong for a human, fitted against his perfectly. For a moment, just one, Q forgot where he was, reveling in how it felt after so many years, to find the one who was right for him. A random chuckle and the blast of a car horn had him pulling back.

"I do like the way you shut me up," Sully said, his blue eyes sparkling in the reflected light of a street lamp. "But now you need to talk because I should warn you, I didn't sign up for a man with a list of rules as long as my arm."

"There're only two." Q slipped off his jacket and put it on the ground, indicating Sully should sit. He handed out the food and for a while, all that could be heard was the rustle of burger wrappers and the soft moans of appreciation. Sully knew the best places for food. It was good.

"Wolves are extremely possessive of their mates," Q said after he'd licked the last of the sauce off his wrapper. Sully was still eating, but his raised eyebrows indicated he was listening. "We live very long lives, and no, before you say it," he added as he saw Sully's eyebrows dip into a V, "when claimed, for the most part, mates live as long as we do. There are exceptions," he thought of Ian, "but as a rule, a human life extends to match ours."

His mouth full of fries, Sully nodded. "We think, although I am not sure anyone knows for certain, a mate is a gift from the Fates; a blessing if you will because we live such a long time. We can pass in the human world, but we age very, very slowly, and so do our mates," he said quickly as Sully opened his mouth again. "It means moving around every ten to twenty years; changing our identities and that can be a lonely life if you don't have someone to share it. It doesn't matter to us what gender or species our mate is, once we find them, we treat out mates like the gifts they are. A shifter won't ever hurt their mate, lie to them, cheat on them – that's not even possible. A mate is the crucial center point in a shifter's life."

"Don't wolves traditionally live in a pack?" Sully had finally finished eating and was sitting with his elbows resting on his crossed legs, his chin on his fists.

"Many do," Q hadn't thought about his pack in years. "Alpha wolves like me, Richard or your friend Zander, often leave because too many alphas in a pack can cause problems. My pack was originally from Montana; I enlisted when I was eighteen and haven't been back."

"How many years ago was that?"

Q was pleased his mate caught on fast. "About fifty. I was a soldier in seven armies before I became a Marine."

Shaking his head, Sully grinned. "Cradle snatcher," he said. But then his face turned thoughtful. "So, given you're a career man and all, I'm guessing a claiming between you and me means we'll spend most of our time apart."

Q winced. "That's not possible. Wolves can't be away from their mates for more than a matter of hours. Anything more and it can become painful; our wolf side gets so distraught we'd just shift and track our mates down, no matter where they were."

Sully's hands and head slumped. "Right; well, I knew this was too good to be true. Will you be okay? I remember Zander telling me even though he hadn't claimed Terry yet, he still couldn't be with anyone else. But I thought that was because Terry was a wolf too."

"That's an alpha/omega pairing," Q said, puzzled by Sully's change of attitude. "I'm not sure what I said wrong. I thought you wanted to hear about shifters and mating. I'll have to go back when my leave's up, but that's only to file my discharge papers. Even if you refuse me now, I'll be a pest until I wear you down.

I'm not walking away from you now I've found you."

"But you're a Marine. A Gunnery Sergeant. I looked that up. That's a freaking important position. Your men depend on you."

"And when I leave they'll depend on someone else," Q replied, determined not to mention how hard it was for him to come to his decision to leave. "A mate is everything to a shifter. There's nothing I won't do for you."

Night had fallen completely now, but thanks to his animal half, Q could see Sully's face clearly. "Would you think any less of me, if I resigned too and we went and did something else, somewhere else?" Sully said finally, his voice low.

Yes! Q did a mental oorah. That had been the next part of his discussion. "I think it's a great idea."

Sully flopped on his back, his arms over his head, a tantalizing strip of skin showing between shirt and jeans. "I know you have a rule, but I need to tell you this and then I promise I'll never speak of it again, okay?"

You're going to tell me you've been nothing but a slut and you'd rather move out of town so meeting all these women won't hurt me. But when Sully opened his mouth, Q's mouth dropped open. *I didn't expect that.*

Chapter Seven

"I was a rampant homophobe. Couldn't stand to be around anyone remotely gay; they reminded me of everything I thought I couldn't have. I was extremely vocal about it; scared someone would notice that I was eyeing asses instead of boobs. I was so bad, when I saw Zander, my best friend, in bed with Terry the morning after he claimed him, I pulled a gun on him and worse, later that morning I filed a false sexual harassment complaint with Internal Affairs against Zander." Sully stared at the night sky, his worst secret exposed. He felt curiously lighter and yet resigned all at the same time. His mate was a Marine and a shifter; there's no way he'd accept him, knowing Sully had blatantly lied to get his friend into trouble. But Sully was done running from himself. It was time for him to admit his mistakes and move on.

"What did you hope to achieve by doing that?" There was no judgment in Q's tone, but Sully carried enough of his own.

"I don't know," he said, exasperation leaking through his voice. "I was angry, hurting. Me and Zander double-dated for years; I never dreamed Zander was interested in males. He never said anything; his ladies were always looking for a second date. And when I saw him with Terry…."

"You felt betrayed," Q moved closer and Sully felt a warm hand on his leg. "You thought Zander should have confided in you; told you the truth about himself, allowing you to do the same."

"Yes…no…I don't know," Sully thumped the ground. "I wanted to hurt him. You should've seen his face; well, before he turned into a four-legged furry. He didn't care. He just blatantly said he'd been with men for years and he just hadn't told me about it. And Terry, curled up in a blanket, defending Zander even though they barely knew each other. I was his best friend. He should have told me."

"You did something stupid. You lied about that day. It split up your partnership and now you're working with guys who act just like you used to."

"Yep. Fitting punishment I guess. Hopefully, it won't result in more than a beating. Of course, I could accidentally end up in the line of fire, but it'd be no more than I deserve." Sully shook his head, the grass prickling his scalp. "I was a fucking asshole. I have been for years."

"Why?"

Good question. Q had no way of knowing what he'd gone through with his father. Glad the darkness hid his face, Sully explained about his younger days, his father's threats to disown him and how he'd used women as a cover since his days in the academy. How lately the pressure had intensified. His father wanted him to marry and have children and how, even now, refused to accept Sully's repeated assertions he was gay.

"It's a sad thing when a parent wants you to live your life as a lie rather than accept you for who you truly are," Q said quietly. By this stage, he was lying beside Sully, the pair of them watching the stars. Even though Sully couldn't see his face, he was comforted by his presence.

"I'm an adult now," Sully replied, his mind working overtime. "If my father can't accept me, then he doesn't. The weird thing is I'll miss them both. My mom, she was always someone special."

"Then chances are she'll find a way to stay in your life. This business with your team bothers me, though." Sully felt his hand lifted, a hard thumb caressed his fingers.

Sully shrugged. "I'm not a quitter. Oh, I know after spilling my sorry tale, it probably sounds like I've been running all my life. But when faced with physical danger, I've never backed down. It's a worry though; if the team splits because of me, then that'll impact our ability to do our job."

"You have to trust the guys guarding your back," Q agreed, "otherwise you can't focus on your job properly. That can lead to mistakes and when firearms are involved, those mistakes can be fatal."

"You sound as though you speak from experience." Sully rolled on his side, laying a hand on Q's chest. "Was it bad?"

"It was a long time ago," Q said quietly. "Before my time in the Marines and it didn't even involve a gun. But it was a death I'll always carry with me. Loving men was a sin and illegal back then and in the armed forces, it was never discussed.

But yeah, there was a guy I trained with. Pushed into the Army by his dad in the hopes it would make him a man. Poor damn fool. Eugene, his name was. Straight off the farm; too naive to hide his nature. He didn't make it through training."

"What happened?" Sully got the impression this was more than a case of a man being in the wrong place at the wrong time.

"Hung himself," Q turned his head and Sully was shocked to see a silent tear run down hardened cheeks. "He couldn't cope with the slurs, the beatings, the accidents and he knew he couldn't go back home. I kept an eye on him; did what I could, but after a couple of weeks we got split into teams and were separated. I asked a couple of other guys to watch his back, but it wasn't enough. I didn't know he was dead until a few days afterward. It was all hushed up. His parents didn't even claim the body. Sent word they were disgraced by their son and wanted no part of it."

"You paid for his funeral." Sully knew that's exactly the type of thing the stoic Marine would do.

"He was a good man with his whole life ahead of him; he didn't deserve what happened to him." Sully laid his head on Q's broad chest, hearing the steady thump of his heart. Q's arm came around him as the bigger man continued. "I've seen death of all kinds; the shitty things people do to each other. So many innocent people caught up in violence that has nothing to do with them; war, famine, civil unrest. Hate is at the root of all of it. Hate stemming from ignorance or fear. I've never understood it. Just tried to do my job and follow orders; praying all the while that one day I wouldn't have to. That one day there wouldn't be another hot spot; there wouldn't be another senseless war."

"And now?"

"I think fifty years' service is enough, don't you?"

Sully nodded, his arms wrapped tightly around Q's body as the man stared at the sky. There were no words he could say that would take away the years of horrors Q had seen. He could only imagine the strength it would've taken to keep going back. He pressed closer, hoping the warmth of his body would be enough.

/~/~/~/~/

Damn it, shit and fucking hell. Q had a strong feeling he'd broken some dating etiquette. On the one hand, he was pleased his mate was so open with him. It took a lot of courage to admit a mistake, especially one as egregious as Sully's. Sully had to have known his admission would make him look bad, but he said it anyway. That was the type of honesty Q appreciated. But now Q was torn. His mate's body was warm against his. It would be so easy to roll over, taste those luscious lips again and claim the man so hard he'd never have any doubt who he belonged to.

But...a Marine never shirked his duty and Q had a duty now to help Sully with the mess he'd gotten himself into at work. Being on the SWAT team was hard enough without worrying if the men with you had your back. If the situation had been any different, Q would've backed Sully's idea to hand in his resignation and be done with it. But now he knew the background, Q wondered if maybe Sully needed to deal with his team and his newly outed status.

If he runs now, he'll always regret it. "Do you have a problem being seen with me as a date in town?" He asked, breaking their comfortable silence.

"I agreed to go out with you, didn't I?"

Hmm, answering a question with a question. "I'm worried about your teammates." Q decided to be honest. "I know you've suggested resigning, but it sounds like, until the last couple of months, you've enjoyed your job."

Sully pushed up and seconds later, Q was staring at the man now straddling him. *Oh, fuck, I'm going to cream my jeans if he moves.*

"What are you saying? You want me to stay in my job now? What about you and your job?"

Q tried to get his thoughts together. It wasn't easy. The hardened muscles of Sully's glutes were pressed right over his erection which hadn't gone down since he'd picked Sully up. "I was thinking we could run a horse ranch," he said through gritted teeth. He slammed his hands over Sully's hips, holding the man still. "We can go looking tomorrow if you like, but I don't want you leaving your job until you're ready. I don't want you to feel pressured."

Sully grinned and Q felt a shiver run down his spine that had nothing to do with fear. His suspicions were confirmed when Sully leaned over him; hands cupping his neck, Sully's breath warm on his face. "You want me," Sully purred.

"I want you safe," Q managed to get out before Sully's lips were on his and his brain synapses fried. Sully was a masterful kisser and with their chests together, Sully's ass parked right over his cock, Q's body burned. His fingers moved of their own volition, tracing Sully's crack through his jeans. *Gods, I want in there,* but the sudden squeal of a police siren had both men freezing.

"Not here," Sully said, jumping up and holding out his hand. "It's time for you to take me home so I can invite you in for coffee." His brain still fuddled with lust, his wolf howling at him to stake their claim, Q took the hand offered and climbed to his feet. He shook out his jacket while Sully collected their trash, yet all the way back to the car, and on the drive back to Sully's, all Q could wonder was how in the heavens name did he lose control of their situation. Weren't they supposed to be coming up with a plan to sort out Sully's job?

Chapter Eight

This has to be the strangest first date ever, Sully thought as he unlocked his door and ushered Q inside. He should know – he'd been on enough of them. Many of the women he'd dated had hinted at "future" talks that included children, living arrangements, and hopes of marriage. That was usually a sign Sully overstayed his welcome. He was getting wedding demands from his father; he didn't need them from his dates as well. But Q was his. It was a Fate thing, or whatever, but Sully knew that in the next hour, sooner if he could get Q naked, his life was going to change forever.

"Did you want that coffee?" He asked, switching on the lights and turning to face Q who was looking around the room. "Or would you prefer something hotter? Me, for instance?"

"I'll claim you if I fuck you now," Q growled and Sully found himself herded against the nearest wall.

"I know." Sully looped his arms around Q's thick neck.

"There's no going back; no changing your mind." Q shuffled closer until not even a breeze could get between them.

"My mind's made up."

"We should talk about your job; I can help."

"Or you can stop talking altogether and kiss me." Sully held his breath. There were flashes in Q's eyes, something not human, but he wasn't afraid. His instinct, something that had never let him down, told him Q would never hurt him. He waited and waited and waited for what seemed like an interminable long time before Q slowly bent his head. The instant their lips touched, Sully let out the breath he was holding, knowing in his soul, he'd found his forever.

Q's kisses became savage and Sully relaxed against the wall. This was it. This was what he'd been missing all his life; someone to take control of his body and wring as much pleasure out of it as possible. Q was doing a fine job. In no time at all he was naked, and thanks to his efforts, Q's neatly pressed shirt was rumpled against his arms, his pants caught on his thighs.

"Lube's in the bedroom," he whispered as Q mounted an oral assault on his collarbone, his thigh caught between Sully's legs creating such delicious pressure.

"Lead the way." Q stepped back and Sully slipped past; a bounce in his step as they covered the short distance from living room to master bedroom. He rustled around in his dresser, snatching up the tube he was looking for.

"No one's been in here," Q said, bending to unlace his boots.

"How did you...oh yeah, wolf senses." Sully's cheeks burned. "It's never a good idea to bring people home unless you want to keep them."

"I don't want to think about what you did before," Q straightened and Sully gasped. Q in clothes was dominating, hard and every inch a Marine. Naked, he didn't lose that military bearing, but damn he was drool-worthy. Not a single hair marred the perfectly sculpted body. Clearly defined bronzed muscles rippled as Q stalked towards him. A broad chest sloping down to a trim waist; thick thigh muscles that flexed with every step and a cock that easily exceeded the size of the dildo Sully pondered earlier. A full sleeve graced one arm; an intricate mass of tattoos Sully knew he'd spend hours studying.

Sully held up the lube, trying not to gulp. "Should I do this or do you...?"

"Get on the bed." The lube was snatched from Sully's hand and praying his nerves didn't show, Sully climbed on the bed. It was one thing to dabble with toys; quite another to anticipate being penetrated by a force of nature.

Moving to lie on his stomach, Sully was surprised when Q flipped him over like he was a featherweight. "I need to do this," Q explained and seconds later Sully moaned and fisted the covers as 'this' proved Q had no gag reflex. His cock encased in suction, Sully lifted his legs as he felt fingers moving over his perineum, holding under both his knees to give Q more room to explore. A pillow was stuffed under his butt while Q proved sucking wasn't his only skill. Teeth grazed across his tightening scrotum and Sully cried out as he felt a tongue run across his hole.

Clearly pleased with his reaction, Q did it again and again. Sully pulled on his knees, his stomach muscles complaining at the squish, but that was something Sully could work on later. For now, his head was tossing back and forth, his eyes closed as he received his first ever rimming experience. Gods, he was glad he had a thorough shower before he went out.

Q's finger was warmer than anything he put in his ass before, but Sully quickly got used to the intrusion. His mind played with the idea of introducing Q to his toy collection, but damn it, the man didn't need any help. It seemed like no time at all and Sully was panting as four fingers were moving easily in and out of his ass.

"Now," he bellowed, sure his body couldn't take the tension any longer. A moment's emptiness and then something thicker was pushing against his hole. Sully blew out and pushed out as Q loomed over him; his arms framing Sully's head.

"Just a bit more, just a wee bit more," Q crooned as Sully started to pant. He was full; fuller than he'd ever been. He could feel his muscles stretching, trying to accept the persistent length that seemed to go on without end. Just when he thought he couldn't take anymore; when he had visions of Q's cock brushing his throat from the inside, Q stopped and Sully was conscious of the man's thighs brushing against his inner thighs.

"I knew you could take me," Q's lips stretched in the facsimile of a smile. "Built for me; made for me and you feel fucking perfect."

"Move." It came out as a whisper but Sully never doubted Q could hear him. The intensity of Q's eyes as they bore into his had Sully feeling strangely vulnerable. He stared back determined to be emotionally open with a partner for the first time in his life. Q gave an imperceptible nod and slowly flexed his hips.

Sully bit the inside of his lip; he could feel his body stretch and then grab as though unwilling to lose the length inside him. Resting his hands on Q's biceps he closed his eyes and focused on the way his body responded. The press of his spine against the mattress, the graze of Q's hips against the inside of his legs; the way his balls tingled every time Q slapped home. His cock was flailing madly on his abs; catching on the smear of precome leaving a trail across them. Sliding his hand down, he grabbed it, his body instinctively arching but he was pinned down.

Tightening his legs around Q's waist he tugged and pulled; his strokes matching Q's ever increasing thrusts. His eyes open now, Sully could see Q's head was bowed, the veins in his neck standing out as his hips beat a merciless tattoo on Sully's behind. Q looked up; his lips curled back revealing impressive fangs. Sully instinctively tilted his neck as far as he could, his heart pounding at the thought of being bitten.

He didn't have to wait long. With a roar, Q's hips snapped against Sully's butt and he struck, the long teeth sliding through Sully's skin easily.

Sully braced for the pain but it was over in an instant. Instead, he felt every cell in his body come alive with lust and he cried out as his cock spurted. He lay trembling, his limbs frozen as Q's teeth were still in his neck; his orgasm still pinging through his body. Completely overwhelmed, Sully barely registered the warmth coating his insides as his world went black.

/~/~/~/~/

Q groaned as he carefully slid his teeth from Sully's neck; taking care to lick the wound thoroughly. He'd felt Sully's body go limp and figured it really wasn't acceptable to keep biting the man when he was unconscious. He couldn't resist a final thrust before slowly pulling out; his cock still half-hard. Not able to remember the last time he'd got any relief, he was keen for another round. But he climbed off the bed after making sure Sully would be comfortable when he woke up.

I should close his legs, but damn if the sight of his come trickling from Sully's ass didn't make him hard all over again. Forcing his eyes away from the delicious picture, he went through the house silently, checking windows and making sure the front door was locked securely. Finding the bathroom, he shook his head at the damp towel lying on the floor and the mess of products on the small counter. *Guess you were in a hurry to get ready,* Q thought, sure his inner smirk was showing.

Hunting through the cupboards he found a couple of washcloths, using one to clean himself then dampening the other to take to his mate. His wolf was a little sad their mate wouldn't be able to mark him; but his body and wolf radiated serenity that had never been there before. *I have a mate! I should tell someone, but who to call?* Q's mind immediately went to Dave, one of his platoon sergeants and someone he'd gone through the ranks with. Dave and he had been on four tours together and out of anyone, Q trusted him most.

He's not going to understand about mates though. While the men who knew him best didn't care who he had warming his bed; they'd all gone through too much to be worried about petty details that had nothing to do with how a man handled himself under fire; no one knew he was a shifter. Q tidied Sully up, tucked the covers over him and climbed into bed after snagging his phone.

There was only one person he could call. He glanced out the window. It was late, but Richard would still be up. Sure enough, the phone only rang once before it was answered.

"You okay, bro?" Richard's quiet voice implied he had company.

"I claimed him." Q knew he didn't have to explain the implications of those three little words. Not to his brother.

"I am so damned pleased for you, bro," Richard's voice was warm and happy. "Big responsibility, do you think you're up to it?"

Q knew his brother was teasing. "Still got a few things to work out, but yeah, I think I'll manage."

"I'm glad you met him, Q; I might get to see a bit more of you, now," Richard's voice dropped and Q heard the rustle of covers. "I have to admit Sully wasn't my favorite person, but if anyone can bring the good out in him, then I know it will be you."

"He told me what he did to Zander. All of it."

"The gun *and* the complaint? I'm surprised he was so honest about it; but hey, that's good. Shows he's got a streak of honor in there somewhere. He's a good detective, provided you weren't gay. The Divas at Club Blue don't like him much."

Q growled. "He made mistakes. Now he's living with them. His team is causing him problems because he's been seen with you and your friends. I didn't want him in that damn job anyway, but I don't want to see him beaten or shot when he's trying to live true to himself now."

"It's okay," Richard said soothingly. "I know you want to protect him. That's the way things should be. But there's not a lot you can do about his issues at work."

Sully stirred and flung out his hand; Q immediately took it and his mate settled, tugging Q's hand to his chest. "I have to go," Q said quietly. "I know what you're saying but a Marine never gives up."

"Start looking online for that ranch of yours," Richard suggested, "and bro, you know I've got your back. Congratulations on your mating."

Q grunted and disconnected the call. Sliding the phone onto the table by the bed, he snuggled down, gently easing Sully into his arms. He felt right there and Q breathed out and closed his eyes. He'd get used to sleeping with someone and being in a strange bed didn't bother him, especially when all he could smell was his mate. Lulled by Sully's scent, Q quickly fell asleep.

Chapter Nine

"No, no, no, no, no." Sully could hear the distant sound of his alarm sounding and his arm flailed out, reaching for where it usually was on the nightstand. But he encountered a wall of flesh instead. "Oops," he said as he opened his eyes to see Q watching him; the memories from the night before flooding his brain. He managed a smile. "Morning. Excuse me a minute. Let me turn that damn thing off." He scuttled out of bed, well aware his ass was flashing as he dashed from the room.

His clothes were still in a pile where he left them, and he pulled his phone from his pants pocket, grimacing at the notification on his screen. Latham wanted to see him ASAP; so much for a quiet morning getting to know the new man in his life. Hurrying into the kitchen, he flicked the switch on the coffee machine and then went back into the bedroom, his feet faltering at the sight of Q sitting up, his muscles gleaming against the pale bedcovers.

"I'm so sorry. I was going to call in sick today, but my boss wants to see me," he said as he flicked his cock down. *I don't have time for that.* "Will you be all right? I don't mean to cut and run like this, but I've put the coffee on. You can stay here if you like. I'll get back as soon as I can."

"I'll take you to work." Q climbed out of bed.

The word "no", hovered on Sully's lips, but he swallowed it down. The ache on his shoulder was a clear reminder of how much his life had changed in the last twelve hours and it was time for him to stop running scared. "That'd be great," he said instead. "If you don't mind hanging around while I have a chat with Latham, we'll get some breakfast afterward."

"I'll just get some clean clothes from the car." Q headed for the door and then turned back, pulling Sully close. Before Sully could take a breath, Q's lips were on his and by the time Q had finished, no amount of punching was going to make his cock go down. "Good morning," Q said gravely, turning for the door again.

"Hey, clothes," Sully called out. "You can't run around this neighborhood naked; you'll scare the kids."

Q's cheeks took on a pink tinge, but the man snatched his pants from the floor and pulled them on; not that they hid much. Sully averted his eyes, rummaging through his closet for a pair of jeans, one of his black tee shirts and a suit jacket. SWAT members weren't expected to wear suits, the way he did when he was a detective, but Sully still liked to look smart. By the time he'd run a comb through his hair and pulled on his boots, Q was back, his tight black tee and jeans leaving nothing to the imagination.

"All set?" Q asked.

"Coffee," Sully said, holding up a finger as he adjusted the holster under his jacket. "Travel mugs in the cabinet above the machine. I take mine black with three sugars. Sugar's in the bowl next to the machine. Spoons are there too."

Q's eyes scanned him like an x-ray from top to bottom before he nodded and left the room. "Okay, okay, got to be organized. Keys, wallet, gun, ID, yep." He slapped the relevant pockets. "Time to face the world as a mated man." *I guess that's kinda like being married,* and silly though that thought might be, Sully had a wide smile as he left the house; Q by his side.

/~/~/~/~/

Q sat ramrod straight in the hard chair, totally ignoring the chaos around him. Sully hadn't said much on the trip to the station, but when Q turned off the engine, he asked if Q wanted to come, and of course, Q got out of the car. Sully was well known;

90

plenty of people waved or stopped to say hello. If he was stopped, Sully introduced Q as his partner, complete with rank, seemingly not noticing the weird looks he was getting. But Q noticed and his wolf was angry; wanting to come out and savage anyone who looked at his mate the wrong way.

It wasn't any easier waiting outside Latham's office. Through sheer will, Q focused only on what was going on behind the door. Words like incompetent and distracted were being spoken in harsh tones, and Q's skin crawled as he fought the need to protect his mate. Sully's voice was respectful when it was heard at all, but when Latham mentioned the word "faggot" Sully's voice came through loud and clear.

"With respect, sir, who I spend my downtime with has no bearing on how I do my job."

"You filed a complaint about your former partner because he tried to seduce you."

"I withdrew that complaint after speaking with Detective Samuels. It was a misunderstanding; one he's forgiven me for."

"I don't care what he's forgiven you for; SWAT members do not run around flaunting their aberrant behavior in public."

"Are you suggesting my relationship with Gunnery Sergeant Thorne comes under that term, sir?"

"I'm suggesting you start acting like one of the team, Detective. I've read your record. I agreed to give you a place because of the number of complaints filed against you by the faggot few in this community. We don't hold with homosexuality in Texas, Detective. Do I make myself clear?"

"Yes, sir. Is that all sir?" Outside the room, Q felt a sting of pain and looked down to see his claws dug into his palms. He wiped them on his jeans, thankful for black pants. The door opened and Q stood, getting a quick glimpse of an older man with a red face, and thinning hair sitting behind a desk before Sully came out. His mate reeked of misery and his smile was forced.

"Ready for breakfast?" Sully asked, not waiting to see if Q answered and heading down the corridor to a marked exit. "Personally, I need a breath of fresh air."

"Does that happen often; him talking to you like that?" Q asked as they walked down the street. Sully seemed to know where he was going; not that it mattered to Q. He wanted to pull his mate close and offer him some comfort. Words were a poor relation to comforting actions. But Sully's body language said it wasn't a good idea.

"You heard all that, did you?" Sully visibly relaxed as though glad he didn't have to rehash it. "Not to me, but then you heard him. Apparently, my skills had nothing to do with my placement with the SWAT team. He thought I'd fit in and now he's rethinking his decision. Who knew being gay affected your ability to assess a situation and point and shoot when ordered?"

Q snorted. "If that was the case, I wouldn't have lasted ten minutes in the armed forces."

"Pain in the ass," Sully muttered and Q assumed he was talking about Latham. "Still, it's good to know where I stand. I thought the conflict would come from a few team members; I didn't realize command was in on it too."

Q wanted to ask if that meant his mate was going to resign his position, but Sully chose that moment to enter a diner. A quick sniff let Q know this was another place that served great food and neither of them said

anything until their orders had been
taken and their coffee mugs filled.

Chapter Ten

"I'm sorry." Sully looked down at his mug and then up at Q. The man's dark blue eyes hadn't left him since he'd got out of Latham's office. "Not an auspicious start to our relationship."

"Relationships aren't only about the good times or the sexy times," Q said quietly. "I'd be a piss-poor partner if I ran off at the first sign of trouble."

"Yeah, and I know you wouldn't do that." Sully's head was a mess. He knew how important being focused on the job was; especially in SWAT. One moment's inattention could be dangerous for everyone concerned. He thought back over his last engagement. Yes, he'd been thinking about Q, but not while he was at the scene. In fact, he'd made a point of not thinking about the delicious looking man. The more Sully thought about his actions the surer he was he didn't put a foot wrong. "It's a real mess. I don't know how much you heard, but I didn't fuck up on the job. I didn't."

"It's okay." Q reached out and covered his hand; Sully's shoulders slumped; something a small part of his brain registered as weird. After spending years hiding who he was; to be essentially holding hands with another man at a local diner, three blocks from the precinct, Sully found he didn't care. He hadn't seduced Q because he wanted to scratch an itch. He wasn't going to ignore his new partner in public.

"I don't know what to do," Sully confessed. "If I quit now then…."

"Your coworkers will assume you're running scared." Q nodded and then sat back as the waitress came with their meals. Her eyes widened as she took in Q's huge frame and their joined hands.

"Thank you for your service," she said to Q, putting their plates on the table.

"How did you know my friend's in the armed forces?" Sully figured in his plain clothes Q could pass for anything from an assassin to a biker, especially with his tattoos on full display.

"Boy, I bet your man screams Marine when he's naked," the waitress winked. "Enjoy your meal."

Sully chuckled as the waitress walked away. The splash of color on Q's cheeks made him look younger, but he didn't say a word, simply picking up his knife and fork and enjoying the food while it was hot.

Quit or stay; quit or stay. No matter how much he weighed things up, Sully couldn't think of a way to keep his reputation, his mate, and his job. The logical thing would be to quit. He had Q now; they could build a life together once Q signed his papers. If it hadn't been for Gibson's comments the day before, and Latham's earlier, he'd have written the letter already.

"What do you know about ranching?" Q asked, placing his knife and fork neatly on his plate and then pushing them aside.

"Er...nothing. I can ride a horse, but I've lived in cities all my life," Sully was so caught up in the merry-go-round in his head he almost missed the question. "Why, do you think I'd look good as a cowboy?"

"You look good doing anything," Q deadpanned. "I'd been thinking about it a lot while I was away. I don't get to run when I'm overseas and I used to spend my evenings dreaming about a huge spread of land; no guns, smog or people yelling all the time. Somewhere where people can be free to be themselves. What do you think?"

By run, Sully was sure Q was talking about the four-legged kind. He was curious about Q's wolf, having only seen glimpses in his eyes. "I think if we tie up our loose ends, it wouldn't hurt to see what's available.

Wherever we go though, I insist on a porch, with a swing or a glider."

"To watch the sunrise?" Q's facial muscles relaxed slightly. Sully was learning that was Q's version of a smile.

"I was thinking more sunsets, but yeah, whatever you fancy. Not sure how we're going to afford it though. I could sell the house." Sully had some savings; he actually had a trust fund, but he was never allowed to touch it. He took pride in knowing the money he saved came with no strings attached.

"Richard's invested my salary over the years; we'll have plenty. You should only sell the house if you want to."

"My sugar daddy," Sully teased, but then his face fell. "I still don't know what I'm going to do about my job."

"How about we go and see a real estate agent and look at some housing options. We don't have to move right away."

"Or," Sully took in his mate's handsome features and felt his cock stir, "we could look at places online. I've got a laptop and we haven't made the bed yet."

"Are you expected back at the precinct?" Q asked, pulling out his wallet and leaving cash on the table.

"I'm on call," Sully said. "I'm not scheduled for another two days and I completed my monthly training Monday. All I would have been doing today was workouts with the team. I can do that with you. Unless something major happens, I'm free till Sunday night."

"Workouts?" Q asked as Sully waved to the waitress and they left the diner. "I'm not the type to go easy on you."

"It could be fun. Hand to hand combat. Naked." Sully winked, watching as Q's eyes glowed.

Uncaring who saw them, Sully caught Q's hand and they headed for the car and then home.

Chapter Eleven

"I need your advice." Q shut Richard's office door and took the closest seat.

"Hello to you too, brother of mine." Richard looked up with a smile. His desk was littered with papers and with his shirt sleeves rolled up and his tie loosened, Q knew his brother wasn't expecting clients. Not that he would on a Sunday. "I thought you'd still be in the mating thrall and didn't expect to see you for at least a week."

"Sully had to go back to work this evening. I dropped him off about an hour ago."

"Your wolf will get used to the separation," Richard said, his voice soft. "It won't be easy, but Sully will be back in your arms in a matter of hours."

"It's not that." Q gripped the arms of the chair, trying to keep his wolf in check. "I expected some angst; gods, I've had a lifetime coping with things

I don't like. And it was fine. I drove away; it was all good. I thought I'd get something to eat and then bam; halfway through a freaking burger, I started sweating and...shit. I think something's wrong with Sully."

"What does he say, you know, up here?" Richard tapped his temple.

"Excuse me?" Q didn't have a clue what his brother was talking about.

"Your mind link. You know; The ability to talk to each other telepathically."

"We have a mind link?" Q had never heard of it before.

"You should have. You mean you've never noticed? I had one with Ian; Zander has one with Terry. You should have one with Sully."

"What does it feel like?"

"Oh fuck," Richard sighed. "That's right. You left before Mom gave me the talk. When you claimed Sully, how did you feel?"

"Happy and still horny, but Sully passed out." Q didn't like not knowing something that could impact his mating and couldn't resist teasing his brother.

"Shouldn't have knocked him out with the first bite then," Richard stuck out his tongue. "Now think, this is serious. Afterward, did you feel like there was an odd yet somehow familiar presence in the back of your mind? It should still be there."

Q focused inward. The only thing in his mind at the moment was his wolf pushing to come out. Shoving the angry animal aside wasn't easy, but Q concentrated. "Yep, got it. Now what."

"Magnify it. Bring it forward." Richard threw up his hands. "I'm not sure how else to explain it, but that's your connection with Sully."

"My damn wolf is getting stroppy." Q heard the sound of cracking wood and looked down to see he'd wrecked the arms of Richard's chair. "I can't get a handle on that buzz thing. It's all over the place. Something's wrong."

"Hang on." Richard lifted a finger, pressing the screen of his phone. It rang twice and Zander answered.

"What is it, Richard? I'm in the middle of something here."

"I've got a crazed wolf here," Richard snapped back. "Has the SWAT team been called out?"

"Fuck. Yes. Look, it's utter chaos here. Tell Q to stay away. I'll see if I can find Sully, but I mean it. Q can't be here. There's fire, ambulance, police...every man and his brother. I can't have a rampaging wolf down here too." Zander clicked off and Q growled.

"Where? Where would they be?"

Shaking his head, Richard tapped a button on his desk and part of the wall cabinet slid away revealing a television. Fishing a remote out of his desk, Richard turned it on and Q's heart sank.

"Repeating our top story this evening; officials report there are still five people unaccounted for in the Central Finance Offices. There're reports of a hostage situation on the fifth floor, but negotiation efforts have been hampered by the fire on lower floors. Police say the fire was deliberately lit but won't say why there are hostages in what should have been closed offices. Law enforcement and fire personnel are working to clear the building and Police advise people to avoid the area. We'll bring you further updates as they come to hand."

Richard clicked off the television and grabbed his jacket. "I'll drive, you shift; but Q, so help me, keep your animal half under control."

"You're coming with me?" Q stood and pulled his tee shirt over his head as he kicked off his boots.

"Someone's got to explain your furry ass to the press. You try going in as a marine and we won't get past the police tape. I'll grab your clothes too, but for fuck's sake, I mean it. Keep a low profile."

Q didn't answer; he was too busy shifting. His wolf, who'd spent decades accepting Q had to lead in times of danger, wasn't staying hidden this time. Their mate was in danger and nothing was going to get in his way.

"I'm going to get fined for not having you on a leash," Richard grumbled, but he opened the door and Q shot out of the room; Richard close behind him.

Chapter Twelve

Sully breathed evenly. He had a visual of two armed suspects. Five hostages were on the floor, but the two were berating an older man, who, from the state of his clothes, had been dragged in along with his family. As smoke crept from the stairwell behind him, he silently cursed the asshole who interfered with his equipment. Latham ordered him out of the truck before he could locate his knife and mask.

"Four, hold your position." Latham's voice crackled in his ear. "Two and three are coming up from the other side. Do not engage. Repeat, do not engage."

Sully tapped his earpiece in response. He couldn't see any sign of Gibson or Marsh. His com device wasn't picking up any discussion on movements, or what anyone else could see. All he had in his ear was Latham and that ass wasn't telling him anything. The two subjects were getting angrier, but there was no sign of a negotiator either. *What the fuck is going on?*

Sully pulled the top of his tee shirt over his nose and mouth as the smoke thickened. A trickle of sweat ran down his brow. If someone didn't move soon, they were all going to fry. Casting another look at the hostages, Sully risked speaking, keeping his voice low. "Sir, perps are getting agitated. Two of the children are coughing badly. I have a clear shot."

"Hold your fire. Gibson and Marsh are in position."

Where? Sully couldn't see them and with the smoke thickening, it was getting harder to see anything at all. Struggling to keep his watering, burning eyes focused through his scope, Sully saw a red spot appear on one of the perp's arm. So did the other perp. Shots rang out and Sully heard one of the little girls scream.

"Going in," he yelled into his mouthpiece, standing to kick in the door.

"Stay where you are," Latham snapped.

"Sir, the children…."

"That's an order."

"The smoke's filling the room," Sully protested. "Those kids…." He ducked as the glass above him broke. Brilliant. Now they were shooting at him.

"Am under fire," he said. "Permission to engage."

There was no reply except the sound of more gunfire. A bullet whizzed past his arm, chipping the door frame. He moved back, coughing. He could hear Gibson's voice yelling for the hostages to exit the room. Standing slowly, Sully's heart dropped as he heard Gibson report. "Two perps down. Hostages on their way out. One man injured in the crossfire. One perp unaccounted for. Permission to sweep the floor."

Permission must have been granted. Gibson and Marsh moved together, back to back, shooting. There wasn't a third suspect. What the fuck were they shooting at? Sully had been in position for fifteen minutes. Gibson and Marsh were wasting a hell of a lot of taxpayers' money, littering the place with spent casings.

"Detective Sully Roberts," Sully stepped forward, his rifle held aloft. "There's no other...." He ducked and ran as both men turned and fired on him. One bullet stung him as it clipped his ear.

"Latham!" Sully yelled as the bullets kept coming. He had no way out. Smoke was billowing up the stairwell. Crackles and pops got louder as the flames got closer. They were on the top floor and if he didn't move soon he'd be stuck. "Latham, you asshole, call them off." There was no reply. He clicked through the channels on his radio but he was getting nothing but static.

"Suspect seen fleeing east," Gibson reported. "Two and three in pursuit."

His heart pounding, Sully searched for a place to hide. His head swam as the smoke rolled around him. Coughs racked his lungs making it harder to move. Fingers of flames licked across the desks and wooden floor. *Windows. Got to find a window or a fucking fire escape.* Disorientated, he dropped to the ground, crawling across the floor, hopefully in the opposite direction to where he'd been. There was no sign of Gibson and Marsh. Sully assumed they'd saved their own lily-white asses.

"Sully!" Zander? It sounded like Zander.

Sully turned to the faint sound of his friend's voice although by now he could see nothing but desk and chair legs.

"Zander, fuck. Get out of here," he gasped as he coughed hard enough to dislodge his lungs. He thought he heard a growl, but it was too low to be human. A shower of bullets decimated the desk he was under. His leg burned. Sully saw a flash of a gas mask. *Gibson.* He tried to scuttle back on his ass. His blood smeared the floor. Framed by flames and smoke, Gibson appeared like a vision from hell; his own personal demon.

Ripping off his mask, Gibson snarled, "You're dead, Fag." He raised his rifle. Sully backed into a corner, his eye's streaming, coughs wracking his body. He shakily raised his rifle, his coughing making holding it steady impossible.

"Don't," Sully groaned as Gibson fired another volley of bullets. He rolled. He heard an inhuman snarl as someone caught him under the arms and dragged him clear.

"Zander?" Sully didn't think he'd ever been so pleased to see his friend. "What?"

"Don't look," Zander growled. "You don't want your first sight of Q's wolf to be like this. We've got to get out of here. The floor's going to collapse any minute."

"Q?" Sully turned back; bile immediately filling his throat. He wretched and choked. "Q! Enough. We have to get Gibson out."

"He tried to kill you and knowing Q, it's too late." Zander hoisted Sully off the floor; Sully screamed as pain shot through his leg. There was a thud of footsteps, the crashing of timbers and floating through the air came an eerie howl. Sully tried to turn; he caught a glimpse of glowing eyes before his world went black.

/~/~/~/~/

"Q, damn it, he's dead, that's enough." Q snarled at the corpse under his paws; the word SWAT emblazoned on the man's vest. Death was the easy way out for an asshole that turned on his own team member.

"We've got to get rid of this body," Richard said, grabbing the prone man's feet and dragging him towards the thick smoke, causing Q to jump off. "Fucking coroner sees him like this and Sully will be in a world of problems." Flames moved steadily across the wooden floor and with a kick, Richard shoved the body right in its path.

How can this be Sully's fault? He doesn't have my teeth.

"Why are you still furry? You have to shift," Richard said urgently as wolf and man ran towards the fire escape. Q didn't listen. Zander had Sully. Another wolf shifter was handling his mate and while yes, he'd be better with two hands, the fire consumed more than half of the floor and now the wolf's instinct was to get the hell out. He wanted his mate with him. He needed him. He caught the hint of fresh air as Richard grabbed him by the scruff and yanked him back.

"Shift back!" Q could scent Richard's anxiety through the smoke. "There're fuckers all around this building. If they see you and that asshole's body doesn't burn, you and I are in shit street. Put your fucking clothes on."

Q knew his brother's words made sense but it was a full minute before he was on his hands and knees panting. He grabbed his pants, wrestled them on and pulled a shirt over his head. Richard silently held out his boots and he yanked them on, hurriedly tightening the laces.

"Zander's got Sully down at the ambulance. His boss is over there now; demanding answers probably. Fuck, I hope your mate's still unconscious," Richard hissed peering out of the window. "We need to get the hell out of here and meet them at the hospital."

"He hasn't gone yet? He was bleeding; I could smell it." Q joined his brother, frowning as he saw the man he remembered from Sully's work trying to stop the ambulance team from leaving. There was a lot of shouting going on and finally, another officious looking man pulled Sully's boss away and with a slam of doors and sirens blaring the ambulance pulled away. Q felt his heart being tugged out of his chest.

"Zander will fill us in when we get there." Richard ducked and then straightened. "Move it, while everyone's attention is on that asshole."

Q glanced over his shoulder as he shimmied down the fire escape. His brother was right; Latham was busy yelling at the man who'd pulled him away from the ambulance and a couple of other men in SWAT jackets were looking angry too. There was no sign of the hostages and the firemen were busy controlling the flames which were pouring from windows on every floor. Blending with the crowds around the police tape was easy as he and Richard dashed towards the car. All the while Q focused on the minute buzz in his head; it was muted to next to nothing. He prayed with everything that he was that the Fates wouldn't be so cruel as to take his mate from him so soon.

Chapter Thirteen

"Q?" Sully's eyes flew open, his hand reaching out instinctively for his mate. White ceiling, beeping monitors. Shit. He was in the hospital.

"I'm here." Q's larger hand engulfed his; the man's voice sounding rougher than usual. Sully turned his head and coughed, his eyes widening as he saw the haggard look on his mate's face.

"How long have I been out?"

"You had surgery on both legs. They removed four bullets."

"Fuck." Sully closed his eyes as the memories flooded back. "The hostages?"

"The children were treated for smoke inhalation. The mom and dad were okay but they are all in hospital overnight for observation."

Thank god for small mercies. It'd killed Sully obeying an order to ignore children in need. He swallowed, the inside of his mouth like a desert. "Gibson?" He managed to croak.

"Missing, presumed dead. Parts of the building collapsed. It'll be a while before anyone finds the remains."

Sully shook his head. He could still see the hatred in Gibson's eyes; the gleam as the man raised his rifle. Then he remembered the growl and the savage way Q took Gibson down. "Thanks," he whispered, his throat still dry.

Q didn't say anything for a long while, prompting Sully to open his eyes. He reached across to the water carafe sitting on the cabinet beside the bed and Q stood, pouring and handing him a plastic tumbler, before sitting again. Sully sipped slowly, his mouth coming alive as the cool liquid slid down his throat.

"Are you okay?" he asked, putting the tumbler back on the cabinet and stroking Q's hand. Q shook his head sharply.

"You got shot."

Sully nodded.

"By a guy who's supposed to have your back," Q growled.

Yeah, it's not as though I'm going to forget that in a hurry.

"Your boss, that fucking Latham is demanding an inquiry. Richard made sure he got a copy of the surgeon's report. The bullets taken out of your leg were police issue."

"They'll claim I got caught in friendly fire. Latham told me to stay where I was." Sully stared at the ceiling. His job was over. He'd be lucky if he got out without being arrested.

"Zander's already onto that. He spoke to the captain and got the transcript of all the recordings. But look, that's not our only problem."

"There's more?" Sully lifted his head staring at his mate in disbelief. "My job is toast; my legs are useless. Now what? Have you been recalled to base or something?"

"No." Q looked at the door. At least Sully had a private room. But he didn't understand when Q went over and locked the door from the inside and then came back, throwing back Sully's covers. "Look."

Sully looked down. His right leg was swathed in bandages; there was another band of white across his left leg. His feet were bare and he wiggled his toes. He didn't feel any pain and prodded the top of his left leg. His nails scratched his skin – he could feel that.

"They removed four bullets?"

It was Q's turn to nod.

"How long have I been in here?"

"Six hours. You were still unconscious when they took you into surgery; four hours in there."

"Two hours in here…." Sully wiggled his toes again and then, in a frenzy of movement, ripped the bandage on his left leg.

"Don't," Q hissed looking over at the door. "Someone will see."

"I need to see, damn it. They took four fucking bullets out of me and I don't feel any pain. It's not…natural," Sully whispered the last word as the bandage came free. There was a mark; bloodstains around a purple mark lined with neat stitches. No sign of any surgical wounds, no cuts, no holes. Nothing.

Looking up at Q who was frowning at his leg, Sully said, "This is because of you? Because we're mated?"

"Increased healing. I'm surprised they didn't notice it when you were in surgery." Q glanced over at the door again. "We have to get you out of here."

"I can see that, but how?"

"Has to be tonight. Quick, under the blankets, eyes closed." Q sprinted across to the door and unlatched it as a nurse bustled in.

"Your friend not awake yet?" Sully heard her ask. He felt fingers checking his pulse and the tightening of the blood pressure cuff. "Hmm. He should be," the nurse said. "He might be sensitive to the anesthetic. Make sure you hit the call button as soon as he opens his eyes. I'll be back in twenty minutes. If he's not awake by then I'll have to call the doctor."

"Yes, ma'am," Q said firmly.

Sully listened as footsteps left the room and Q clicked the lock. "The night shift goes off in an hour. We'll go when everyone is busy with the changeover," Q said and Sully felt the bed dip. Opening his eyes, Q's face was right there, hovering over him like a grumpy angel. "You scared the fuck out of me."

Q's whispered confession blew all thoughts of escape from Sully's mind. He reached up, Q's scruff scratching his palm. In his head, he and Q hadn't been together long enough to have formed a strong bond although he had a powerful attraction to the man. But as he took in the dark bruises under Q's eyes and the look of sheer despair on his ruggedly handsome face; Sully realized for a wolf shifter, that bond was in place from the moment of claiming – maybe sooner, he didn't know.

"Never again," he promised quietly. "I figure four bullets should put me out of a job, don't you think? I'd go crazy if they gave me a desk job."

Q didn't answer; burying his head in Sully's neck, his broad shoulders shaking. Sully cupped his head and ran his other hand up and down Q's arm, holding him as tightly as he could. For a long time, the silence of the room was broken only by the beep, beep, beep of the heart monitor and the slight rattle of the bedframe as Q wrestled with his emotions.

Chapter Fourteen

"Come on, hurry," Q cast another worried look out the door. The morning shift had arrived along with Richard, Zander, and Terry. Zander had clothes for Sully; his uniform was only fit for the trash bin and while Q's wolf was still on high alert and hated that his mate would smell of another wolf, he wasn't in a position to argue. Sully was standing; a bit shaky, but he could walk and that wasn't something Q thought possible in the four hours he'd paced the waiting room.

"Richard, Q and I will head out past the nurses. Terry's got the keys and will go with you, Sully. No matter what happens keep that hood up and keep fucking walking," Zander ordered.

"They're going to have a fit when they realize I've discharged myself," Sully said, shrugging into the oversized hoodie. "Latham's going to be looking for me; I'm surprised he's not here already."

"You can't let a doctor see your legs," Q grumbled, annoyed he couldn't be by his mate's side. But Zander made a valid point. The nurses knew he hadn't left Sully's side. He couldn't be seen walking with him out of the hospital. Terry was an omega; the type to go belly up in any confrontational situation though and that worried him. "Let's get this over with."

With Zander on one side and Richard on the other, Q admitted they made an impressive block, preventing anyone seeing Sully and Terry slipping out of the room. "Sergeant Thorne, heading out for some breakfast?" The cheery nurse who had been on duty smiled as they slowly walked down the corridor.

"Sully's sleeping. I won't be long," Q lied as he kept walking.

"Hospital food won't be enough to fill you," The nurse flirted as they went past. Q tried smiling but wasn't sure he was successful. He felt an itch between his shoulder blades; someone was watching him. Tapping Richard's hand, he kept his eyes forward as Richard turned to look.

"Boys in blue have arrived. Step on it," Richard murmured.

The three men kept their steady pace until they turned the corner. "Stairs," Q ordered as they broke into a run. His keen ears picked up shouting and arguing at the nurses' station.

"Fuck, I'm going to lose my job over this," Zander grumbled as he easily kept pace with Q.

"Should have stayed out of it then." Q's only focus was getting to Sully.

A strong arm whirled him around; fury written all over Zander's face. "He's my friend," Zander snarled. "He wouldn't be in this shit if he hadn't met you."

"No, he'd be dead." Q wrenched his arm from Zander's grasp and headed for the bottom of the stairs. The exit door had shoddy security; a quick flick of the wires with his claws and they were out. "Where's the car?"

"This way," Richard took the lead, crossing the vast parking lot, heading for the road. Despite being early morning, commuter traffic was building up and Q slowed his steps so as not to attract attention even as his wolf was howling at him to find their mate. Recognizing Richard's vehicle, he frowned as he didn't notice anyone in it.

"Sully," he called out at the same time Zander yelled for Terry. Looking around, there was no sign of anyone. Zander snarled and thumped the top of Richard's car hard enough to leave a dent.

"They caught a fucking bus," Zander yelled throwing up his hands.

"They must have had a good reason," Richard said, patting his pockets. "Fortunately, I have spare keys. Get in."

Q wasn't as vocal as Zander; it wasn't in his nature, but by the hell, he was ready to give Sully the spanking Zander was mentally promising Terry as they got in and joined the commuter traffic.

/~/~/~/~/

"Zander and Q are pissed," Terry confided as the bus rattled its way towards Sully's home.

"How do you know that? It takes a lot to get Zander angry." Sully rubbed his legs. Amazed he could walk at all; his muscles were jellified by the time he sat down.

Terry tapped his head, looking at Sully expectantly. Sully raised his hands, palm up.

"The mind link," Terry whispered, leaning close. "Shit, you stink."

"Try getting shot at while trapped in a burning building and see how good you smell," Sully blushed. He didn't like being reminded he needed a shower. "What do you mean mind link?" He dropped his voice although most of the people sharing the bus seemed half asleep. No one was paying attention to a hoodie-wearing grump and his slender companion.

"Didn't Q tell you? Shit, maybe you don't have one." Terry frowned, the furrows on his brow decidedly cute. "Nah. You must have. All couples like us have one. Think something to Q."

"Think something? I think about him ninety percent of the time."

"Think at him." Terry's forefinger rested on his forehead and then flicked out. "As if you were talking to him, but in your head."

"This is nuts." Sully was glad his hoodie covered half of his face. Closing his eyes, he thought hard. *Hey, Q, you there?*

Terry giggled. "You look like you're trying to take a poop."

"Shut up," Sully was going right off his friend's mate. "How will I know...oh."

Sully...Sully...what the fuck are you doing on a bus?

"Gods, this is harder than it should be," Sully whispered to Terry, "but yep, he sounds pissed off."

Saw Latham in the parking lot. Made a detour, he sent or hopefully sent. Sully had no idea how reliable this mental form of communication was.

We're waiting by the bus stop closest to your house.

"Zander's threatened to spank my ass when we get home," Terry said, his eyes bright as he fidgeted in his seat. "You'd think they'd be pleased we showed a bit of initiative."

"Yeah," Sully agreed. "Q forgets I'm a Detective."

"Might not pay to mention that in an argument," Terry whispered. "He...our types...we get really volatile when we see someone we love hurt."

"I doubt Q loves me," Sully said, shocked. "We've barely been together a week."

"You didn't see him at the hospital. Four hours that man paced the floors. Muttering under his breath; jumping on anyone in a white coat that came within ten feet. It was so bad nurses and doctors were avoiding our corridor."

"He did look tired when I woke up."

"It was the not knowing," Terry sympathized. "No one would tell him anything for ages and finally Zander pulled his badge and demanded an update. But nope, his badge didn't work either. Patient records are confidential. Richard finally got a nurse to talk to him; saying that Q and you were close and he'd just got back from overseas to hear his friend had been shot. The number of times Richard had to physically stop him from going into the operating room; it was hell on him and I can understand that."

"It's not as though I planned to get shot," Sully said, although he felt guilty. He should have been more understanding of Q's feelings. Looking out the window, he recognized the neighborhood and stood. A hand on his arm stopped him.

"Being with Q is going to be more intense than any other relationship you can imagine," Terry said softly. "Go easy on him."

"What about you? Worried about your ass turning pink?" Sully grinned as Terry blushed.

"Nah," Terry said with a wink. "Once I have his cock in my mouth he forgets anything else."

A shocked gasp from a woman in the seat next to them had Sully and Terry both chuckling as they got off the bus. Sure enough, Q and Zander were both standing at military rest; Richard was leaning on the car playing with his phone.

"And the race is on," Terry laughed, digging Sully in the ribs as he took off, flying straight into Zander's arms.

Sully followed a little slower; his legs still weren't at full strength. "Did you put the coffee on?" He asked as he wrapped his arms around Q's rigid frame.

"I, for one, could do with some coffee and breakfast." Richard pushed himself off the car. "Come on Zander, let's leave these two alone and see what we can scavenge from Sully's refrigerator."

"I've been more worried in the last twelve hours than I was through two tours in Afghanistan," Q whispered.

"We'll find that ranch," Sully promised. "Somewhere quiet, just you and me. No guns, no work, no one dissing on us because we love each other. Just horses, cows and maybe a few chickens."

"Perhaps not chickens," Q said with that little quirk that suggested he was smiling. "Unless you don't mind replacing them every week."

"Why? Oh...right...no chickens. What about ducks?" Keeping one arm around Q's waist, the two men headed towards his house. "Peacocks? What's your stance on goats?"

"My wolf is loving you right now. You have excellent taste in lunch options."

Sully beamed at the love reference. He already knew Q and his wolf were one and the same. *Maybe a week isn't too soon after all.*

Chapter Fifteen

Q was slicing vegetables for dinner when there was a sharp knock at the front door. "I'll get it," he said, dropping the knife and hurrying through to the living room. "You're supposed to be injured, remember. Back on the couch."

"Oh yeah," Sully grinned as he climbed back on the couch and threw a blanket over his legs. "Better?"

"You still look too damn happy for a person shot in the last twelve hours," Q strode over to the door and opened it. An older corpulent version of Sully in an expensive suit glared at him.

"I demand to see my son." *Well, that answered my first question,* Q thought as he stepped aside. Sully's face was white and his eyes looked as though they were about to fall out.

"Dad. What are you doing here?"

"What do you think I'm doing here? I'm listed as your next of kin. I got a call from your Captain; some nonsense about you being shot. I went to the hospital and they told me you'd discharged yourself so I came around here to see what idiotic stunt you've pulled this time."

"You didn't have to fly all this way in just for that. I...er...I...."

Q couldn't resist the plea in Sully's eyes and hurried to his side.

"Your son was on a mission last night," he said, his voice abrupt. "He was shot; they removed four bullets from his legs. He decided to come home this morning as there is nothing else they can do and I'm looking after him."

"And who the hell are you?"

Mr. Roberts obviously intended to be intimidating but Q wasn't fazed. It was Sully who answered though, his voice strong and clear this time. "This is Gunnery Sergeant Thorne of the US Marine Corps. He's my fiancé. Seeing as you were threatening me with an arranged marriage, I decided to go ahead and marry someone of my own choosing."

Q was glad of his military training. But he wasn't as shocked as Sully's father.

"Marriage? You're going to marry...this...this...."

"Watch it, Dad," Sully's voice lowered. "Q's done two tours in Afghanistan, protecting asses like you. I won't have him disrespected in my home."

Mr. Roberts' face went an alarming shade of red. "I warned you," he snarled. "I've been warning you since you decided to head down your little path of deviancy just to provoke me that I won't have a gay son."

"And I've been telling you since I was fifteen that I'm gay; I'll always be gay. I was born gay and now I've met the man I want to be with the rest of my life, I'm going to marry him." Sully reached out his hand and Q took it, his eyes never leaving the older man. "This isn't about you. It was never about you. It's about me and the way I want to live my life. When will you accept I'm an adult and can live my life my own way?"

Mr. Roberts sneered. "And how long is your precious war hero going to stick around now you've lost the use of your legs? You must have told him about me. Why else would he stick around? If he thinks for one second, he's going to live off my money, then he's sadly mistaken."

"I'm standing right here," Q warned, his temper rising. A quick squeeze from Sully and he adjusted his tone. "I don't know who you are. Sully never talks about you and I can see why. Unless you've got something caring to say about your son who was injured in the line of duty, I suggest you leave. Now."

"You haven't heard the last of this," Mr. Roberts warned. "See how long you last when your soldier boy deserts you and you're left crippled, unemployed and in the gutter. You'll come crawling back. You'll see."

Q pointed to the door and with a last scowl at Sully, Mr. Roberts left; the front door slamming behind him. Sully drew in a shaky breath. "Now you've met my father. Changed your mind about me yet?"

"Who is he?" Q asked. "He sounded as though he expected me to know who he was."

"Senator Arthur Douglas Roberts, New York," Sully sighed. "Very rich. Very well connected and extremely conservative. As you can imagine, I had an interesting childhood. He's the reason I came to Texas for my police training. Even then he kept tabs on me and apparently, things haven't changed."

"What about...." Anything else, Q could have asked was cut off by another loud banging on the door.

"Fucking hell," Sully griped. "Should just leave the thing open and be done with it."

"Stay on the couch." Q stormed over to the door and opened it.

/~/~/~/~/

His head still reeling from the confrontation with his father, Sully's mood didn't get any better when two familiar faces from the precinct walked in as though they owned his house. "Melissa, Croydon. Forgive me for not standing up. I take it this is an official visit? Q, these two are from Internal Affairs. Lieutenant Melissa Williams and Sergeant Croydon. Guys, this is my fiancé, Gunnery Sergeant Quentin Thorne." *If I say it often enough, it might come true.*

"Your fiancé? Times have changed," Melissa smiled as she shook Q's hand and sat down. Croydon stayed standing by the door, his lips pursed as though sucking lemons.

"A lot of things have," Sully agreed. "To what do I owe the pleasure? To be honest, I expected Commander Latham at my door, not you two. Am I under investigation? I only ask because my fiancé's brother is Richard Thorne, the attorney. I'd like him to join us if I'm in trouble."

"You're not in any trouble and Commander Latham has been relieved of his duties pending our investigation into your shooting and the death of Sergeant Gibson. We're here to take down your official statement if you're well enough to proceed that is."

Sully froze, unsure of what to say. "I have to admit, once I got hit, things were a bit of a blur after that. I'm not sure how much help I'll be."

"We understand," Melissa said with a smile while Croydon harrumphed behind her. "I'm surprised to see you out of the hospital so soon. The medical reports showed you were shot four times."

"That's right. Q, my partner, agreed to look after me. Once the bullets were out, I didn't see the point in taking up a hospital bed when I can recuperate just as easily at home."

"Very commendable." Melissa looked down at the sheaf of papers she had in her hand. "Are you aware the four bullets recovered are from Gibson's rifle?"

"I wasn't aware that had been conclusively verified." Sully's mind raced. *How much do I tell them?*

Only the barest details, Q's quiet voice replied. Sully shook his head slightly, still unused to hearing someone talking in his head.

"Ballistics matched the bullets to Gibson's rifle overnight," Melissa looked up from her papers. "One officer shooting another is a serious offense as you are well aware. Any issues between partners and teams are investigated fully."

Thanks for reminding me of our last conversation, Sully thought, keeping his face blank. But then Melissa put him right in a pickle with her next question.

"Did you have any reason to believe Sergeant Gibson shot you deliberately?"

"There was a lot of smoke...the office was on fire. I did identify myself but it's possible Gibson and Marsh didn't hear me."

"Officer Marsh heard you perfectly well. He claimed Gibson fired at you deliberately and that Gibson refused to leave with him when he went to ensure the hostages' safety."

Kiss ass is saving his own butt. Sully heard Q's murmur of agreement in his mind. Out loud he said, "I did try to get in touch with Latham after I knew the hostages were free. There seemed to be a problem with my communications."

"Latham claimed you turned your radio off and refused to follow his orders," Croydon spoke up for the first time.

Sully lightly bit the end of his tongue. "I am confident the audio recordings will prove that's not the case."

"Indeed." Melissa threw a glare at her partner. "Audio recordings show that Latham ordered you to stay at your position despite shots being fired in your direction and the fire making escape difficult. Is that correct?"

Fuck. This is it. This is where I end my career as a whistleblower or let the bastard off.

Tell them the truth. Sully looked over to see Q's eyes focused only on him and nodded. "After the subjects were shot and the hostages freed, I heard Gibson and Marsh tell Latham there was another suspect and they asked permission to continue looking for him."

"Did you see a third perpetrator?" Melissa asked.

"No, I did not and I had a visual on the situation for at least fifteen minutes at that time."

"But it's possible one was hiding in the building somewhere?" Croydon asked. Sully remembered him being a tenacious terrier at the best of times.

"I wasn't aware of one. When shots were fired in my direction, I stepped forward and identified myself. The shooting continued. I asked Latham to notify the officers I was in firing range, but at that point, my communications were cut off."

"The last voice on the recording was yours yelling at your commanding officer to call them off, or words to that effect," Croydon snapped.

"I wonder what tone of voice you would use when you were being shot at by your own team members and this was after your commanding officer insisted you remain in position when you could hear children in distress." Sully refused to let someone like Croydon belittle what happened.

There was silence and then Melissa closed the file on her lap and stood. "Thank you, Detective. I think we have all we need for now."

"Hang on a minute," Croydon protested, moving forward. "This all seems a little slam dunk to me. First, you file a complaint against your partner in Vice complaining he tried to seduce you and then six months later, your own team members are trying to shoot you. Why? Are you that much of an asshole?"

Q growled a distinctly mean sound and Sully said quickly, "Hate, Sergeant. I'm sure you've heard of it. Hate for people who are different. I withdrew my complaint against Zander; told you honestly, I'd misread the situation, which I had. Zander forgave me and we remained friends. I have been out a few times with Zander and his partner Terry since then; it seemed Latham and other members of my team resented my association with the 'faggot few' as Latham called them a few days ago. So, you see, it was hate that left me with four bullet wounds. Now maybe you can see why it took me so damn long to come out of the closet."

He lay back on the couch, his eyelids heavy. "Now, if you don't mind. It's been less than twenty-four hours since I've had major surgery. If there's nothing else, perhaps you'd allow my m...partner to see you out."

"Of course," Melissa said and Sully could hear Croydon grumbling as Q escorted them out. He opened his eyes as he heard the door shut and the lock click. "Did I do all right?" He asked with a smirk.

"You got rid of them which I figured was your main objective. Are you all right, though? You've had a rough afternoon." Q came and sat by his side. Sully shuffled over to give him more room and then sank back into his mate's arms.

"I'm doing okay," he said, realizing it was true. "I don't care what happens to Latham or Marsh. I won't be working with them again. I'll put in my resignation papers while I'm still on sick leave and that will be that."

"And your father?"

Sully nuzzled and then lightly bit Q's neck, a shiver running down his back as Q's arms tightened. "I'll call my mom in a few days and let her know what's going on. I'm sure she'll visit when she has the chance. She's not the type to care about the gender of the person I'm supposedly marrying." He looked up; Q's eyes were dark giving no indication of what he might think about the marrying statement. "She's going to pester you about grandchildren though."

"We'll get the marriage license tomorrow." Q's head bent and Sully felt a broad palm on the back of his head.

Oh yeah, this is what I've been missing.

Chapter Sixteen

Q loved his mate. He wasn't one for flowery words and always believed actions spoke volumes. So, as he kissed Sully he tried to convey the passion in his heart; tried to show how much Sully's defense of him in front of his father and the way he brought up their possible marriage so easily meant to him. Unfortunately, his emotions had gone through the ringer as well and his wolf was pushing for a mount and claim. It was hellishly distracting.

"What's wrong?" Sully pulled back, his blue eyes shining and worry tugging at his lips. "I don't stink like hospital anymore. I had a long shower."

"It's not that." *See,* Q cursed himself, *sometimes actions are misconstrued. Freaking wolf can't have his own way all the time.* "I just...I want...you have to know...willyoutakemethistime?" Q froze, waiting for Sully's response. His eyes widened further, then Sully blinked three times. Q noticed things like that.

"I'd love to," Sully said quietly. "But from the flash of wolf in your eyes, I'm not sure it's a good idea. I take it you don't usually do things that way?"

"You have nothing to fear from my wolf." Q turned Sully around so his mate was straddling his lap. He didn't want to have this conversation but he had to. "I'm sorry for what you saw last night, but believe me, we'd never ever hurt you, no matter what form I'm in."

Sully closed his eyes as though blocking images he'd rather not see and Q cursed himself again for reminding him. "Your wolf is a very powerful animal," Sully said when he finally spoke. "Savage, primal and even though I'll never forget the sight of Gibson's neck torn to shreds, it didn't horrify me and if anyone's surprised about that, it's me. I felt proud."

"Proud?" Q hadn't expected that and his respect for his mate grew.

"You were protecting me. No one's ever done that before."

"But surely Zander, you were on the force together…."

"He had my back the way a partner should," Sully's eyes flew open. "He stood by my side, we protected each other and we were a damn good team. But you…that was personal. I don't know how much you heard…."

"I heard what he called you. I could smell his hatred through the smoke." Q's lips tightened as his wolf surged, remembering all too well the anger he'd felt in that moment.

"And you did what any wolf would do, faced with a threat to his mate." Sully's hand was warm on his neck. "I guess I never really thought about what it must be like to be a shifter until that moment. To live with such a powerful spirit inside of you and yet, so often, forced to live by human rules and regulations." His voice and head dropped. "I realized then what an amazingly special person you are."

"I won't ever let you down." Q knew that as well as he knew his own name but he wasn't sure if that's what Sully wanted to hear.

"I'm just not sure if I'm enough for you," Sully confessed, his head still lowered so all Q could see was the fine blond of his short hair. "I've made so many mistakes; hurt so many people. What if I let you down?"

Gently raising Sully's chin, Q stared into eyes he wanted to see every single day for the rest of his life. "You won't," he said simply. "You have a big heart; you simply need the chance to set it free."

Sully's eyes searched his and then Q was engulfed in frantic arms, Sully's lips hot and hard against his. Through their bond, Q could feel it; joy and passion. As though the confrontation with his father was the cue Sully needed to finally be free to be who he was. A gay man. A mated man. A very horny man.

Quick to catch up, Q groaned as his claws shredded Sully's shirt, his fingers molded to the skin beneath. Lips and teeth smashed together as tongues tangled in an erotic duel that was driving Q out of his skull. His cock ached, caught as it was in the confines of his pants and ensuring he was holding Sully steady, Q stood, making his way to the bedroom.

Sully never let go; if anything, he clung tighter, making Q's steps difficult. Q knew what he said before, but he hoped like crazy Sully had forgotten. He wasn't going to find peace until his cock was sheathed in Sully's body. The urge to possess, to claim increased and he put his claws to work again on Sully's pants this time.

"Bed. Wall. I don't care. Q please," Sully panted as Q's hands cupped

Sully's ass. The wall was a tempting offer. It was right there, but Q didn't have lube and he wouldn't take his mate dry.

"Bed." Two steps and Q managed to pry Sully's hands loose enough to bounce him on the mattress. "Lube." Sully fished under the pillows and held it up. "Pants." Blushing a bright red, Sully tugged off the remains of his pants and threw them on the floor. When he rolled over and kneeled on all fours, Q didn't stop him. He was too busy drooling.

"Get on with it." Sully's voice was muffled by the mattress, but Q heard the command easily enough. Taking just enough time to free his cock, he smeared lube on his fingers before tossing the tube aside.

This is going to be quick.

I don't care. My balls are about to explode.

Still unused to hearing Sully's heated tones in his head, Q's lip quirked as he quickly and efficiently prepped his mate. His focus was honed on one tiny hole. Nothing else mattered although Sully's ragged breathing, the twitches of his skin and the tension in Sully's balls, hanging low between his legs all added to his increasing need.

Finally deeming his mate ready, Q wiped the residue of the lube on his cock and leaned over the bed, tugging Sully closer to the edge. Resting his dick against Sully's crack he thrust a couple of times, loving the warmth of skin combined with the slide of the lube.

"Don't tease. I'll blow without you." Sully's head was resting on the mattress, his back bowed slightly and Q could see his hand was clenched around his cock. He slipped his arm around Sully's chest, effectively knocking his hand away as his other hand guided his dick. A guttural moan escaped his throat as he sank inside. *Too long, it's been too fucking long.*

Move damn it, I'm not made of glass.

Q was quick to comply. The ache in his balls intensified; his thighs trembling with the effort not to ram Sully hard. It'd been more than a full day since he'd had this and he wasn't small as evidenced by the tight squeeze Sully had on him. He moved slowly at first, pushing further with every thrust but as the need overtook him, he sped up. Sully's moans were music to his ears, feeding his lust and spurring him on. He ran his hand down Sully's torso, lightly cupping his cock, the top slick with juices.

"Harder," Sully groaned, rocking back. "I need to feel you."

Knowing how he felt, Q thrust harder. The end was near; the tingle in his stomach, the way his balls tightened. His fangs dropped, grazing his lip and as Q looked down, Sully's neck was right there, his scar pale against tanned skin. *MINE.* Q totally agreed with his wolf and before he could think, his teeth were in Sully's neck.

His mate's body arched beneath him as Sully screamed and a sticky liquid coated his hand.

Damn. Q froze, his cock buried deep inside of his mate, pulsing its release. Sully's blood was warm on his tongue and he carefully pulled his fangs out; he wasn't a vampire after all. But that didn't stop him licking over Sully's wound, or licking his lips afterward. *MATE.* Yes indeed.

Pulling out slowly, Q paused to admire the view once more, before tenderly laying Sully out on the covers. "I'll get a cloth," he muttered, but Sully just gave a sleepy wave. As he hurried to the bathroom, Q wondered if he'd ever get tired of seeing his mate sated among the pillows. His cock didn't think he would.

Chapter Seventeen

Three weeks later

Sully rubbed over the broad platinum band on his ring finger and then looked out of the car window at the military base across the road. Q was in there somewhere, going through his debriefing, saying goodbye to his men. Sully had offered to stay at the hotel but the tightening of Q's lips let him know that was the wrong thing to say. Since their wedding two weeks before; a quiet affair at city hall with just Zander, Terry, Richard and Roy in attendance, Q had been more possessive than ever, if that was possible.

Sully was amazed at how relaxed and comfortable he was in their relationship, finding more to love about his enigmatic mate every day. Q was a man of few words, but Sully learned that everything that came out of his mouth was the truth. While Q didn't verbalize the words Sully longed to hear, his actions spoke of his devotion, his loyalty and his caring. Little things, like making his coffee every morning, picking up his dirty towels from the bathroom without complaint and never failing to hold his hand in public. Their sex was off the charts good and Sully grimaced as he wiggled in his seat. He walked around with an almost permanent reminder of just how much Q desired him.

It wasn't just the little things either. Sully struggled with keeping his injuries, or lack of them hidden; being forced to stay on the couch while his colleagues visited made him feel sick inside. Q soothed him; listened to him rant and then usually took him to bed to pound his frustrations away. Or sometimes the couch. It was quite an effective technique.

His resignation from the job that had been his life was greeted with relief, it seemed, from the powers that be at least. A couple of calls from IA; a condolence visit from his captain. No one from SWAT darkened his door which was probably a good thing given Q's anger at the whole affair. Nothing was said publicly beyond a small newspaper article mentioning a memorial service for Gibson "killed in the line of duty," and a mention of Latham's resignation. Sully's pain at the casual dismissal of someone trying to kill him resulted in an all-night bender with Zander; Q and Terry hovering but doing nothing to interfere. But it was Q who held his head as he paid homage to the porcelain bowl the following morning. Remembering the incident now had Sully shaking his head. There was nothing his mate wouldn't do for him.

The shrill tones from his phone pulled Sully from his reverie. He frowned at the name on the screen. His mom. As promised, Sully called his mother as soon as he and Q picked a date for the wedding. He'd been hurt that his mom said she couldn't attend and basically made it clear she didn't want to talk to him. He'd text a few times since, but the replies were brief and over the past week he'd given up. Rubbing his stomach, bubbling with anxiety, Sully accepted the call.

"Mom, is everything okay? Nothing has happened to Dad, has it?"

"Your dad is as stubborn and as healthy as an ox," his mom said firmly. "I was worried about you. I haven't heard from you for a week. Has that man of yours run out on you?"

"My husband is fine, thank you." Sully looked over at the base gates but there was still no sign of his mate. What should've taken an hour was now into its second and while he knew Q would be safe, he still worried what was taking so long.

"Husband, yes of course. That ridiculous marriage." A long sigh came over the phone. "You know I've always accepted you, don't you? But this is just going too far. Your dad was in a hell of a state when he got back from seeing you. He didn't tell me the extent of your injuries, how long you were going to be in a wheelchair, if you'd ever walk again. The first I heard you'd healed was from your texts. All he could rant about was you marrying a man you barely knew simply to spite him. Sully, why did you do it? How long are you going to persist in this scam? You know your father's not getting any younger and he wants to see you with children of your own."

Sully stared at his screen in shock. "That's why you didn't come to my wedding? Because you think it's a scam to upset dad?"

"Well, no, not exactly." Sully could hear the uncertainty in his mom's voice. "But your dad was adamant about it. Said you were flaunting your boy toy in his face, deliberately trying to hurt him. I know you two have had your differences, but marrying a man out of spite is going too far. I didn't even know you were seeing someone. The last I heard you were going out with Susie and then suddenly you're marrying a man."

Blowing out a long breath, Sully tried to keep his voice calm. "Mom, for one thing, Q is older than I am. He's a Marine and has done countless tours overseas. He's hardly a boy toy. As for flaunting him in dad's face, how was I to know he was even going to turn up? It's not as though I had time to plan any of this scam as you call it. I'd been shot the night before and Q took me home so he could care for me."

"A marine? Your husband is a marine? How...what...oh, damn that man for lying to me. You wait until I get my hands on him." His mother's voice was fierce. "He told me you had a houseful of scantily clad men, and simply pulled one out of the crowd and introduced him as your fiancé."

"There was only me and Q at home when Dad arrived. Believe me, after just getting out of the hospital, I wouldn't have had the energy to entertain a houseful of scantily clad men. I've never had that sort of party." Sully chuckled. "Q's a one-man kind of man and he's not the type to screw around on me."

"It sounds like you really love him." Sully's mom's voice was quiet and Sully wasn't sure if she approved or not. But he was still determined to be honest.

"I do and that's the only reason I married him. Mom, you were the one that told me when you meet that special someone you grab them and never let them go. Q is it for me. He's my life. He means everything to me."

"Oh Sully, can you ever forgive me?" Sully was shocked to hear his mom crying. "I missed your wedding and everything. I'm so sorry. It's just, I've never seen your dad so upset. He had me convinced you were getting married just to annoy him."

"Mom, I've never done anything to deliberately hurt you or Dad. Never. I married Q because I want to spend my life with him. How could you think I'd do something so serious, so life changing and so permanent, to hurt someone else, especially my dad. I'm not like that."

"I know," Sully's mom sniffed. "I know and I should have gone with my gut instinct or at least talked to you properly first."

"I don't hate Dad," Sully risked another look out of the window but there was still no sign of Q. "I've never hated him. I have always just wanted to live my own life, as the gay man I am. This was never a phase, never something I chose to hurt Dad. I was born this way and now finally, thanks to Q, I have the courage to live my life the way I always wanted. I don't understand why he can't be happy for me."

"Your dad is set in his ways," Sully's mom said sadly. "No matter what happens, you will always be his son. He's angry and hurting right now because he doesn't understand."

"Understand what? I'm still his son," Sully blinked back his tears glad for the anonymity the car gave him. "I graduated from the police academy with honors; I became a detective in record time. I own my house and I still watch sports every chance I get. Being married to a man hasn't changed any of that."

"I know, but some people are just too set in their ways to change and you have to accept that side of things too. The best thing you can do is live your life as happy as you are able and over time I know he'll come to accept your marriage. He does love you."

He has a funny way of showing it. "It's okay, Mom, I get it." Sully finally saw Q striding out of the base gates, a large canvas duffle slung over his shoulder. "I have to go. Q's got his discharge papers today. We've bought a ranch just outside of

Hockley; a hundred and fifty acres and a beautiful five-bedroom house. We're moving in two weeks."

"Send me the details; I really want to meet the man who stole your heart. He sounds like a real keeper. I'm still going to expect grandchildren, you know."

"Q's looking forward to meeting you," Sully said warmly. "Thanks, Mom, I'll see you real soon."

He pocketed his phone as Q swung into the car. "Everything go okay? You were longer than I thought you'd be."

"Officially discharged," Q patted the bundle of papers sticking out of his shirt pocket. "I was telling a couple of the guys about our new place. Think you can handle having marines visiting every now and then?"

"Sure, as long they don't expect me to be in a frilly apron and high heels."

Q arched his eyebrow and there was that tug of a smile that Sully had come to know and love. "I think you'd look pretty good in heels," he said with a perfectly straight face. "Now get this baby started. A hot lunch with my hot man and then a flight to Houston. We've got a lot of packing to do at home."

"Have you got a problem with an evening flight?" Sully winked as he started the car. "Those airplane bathrooms aren't big enough for both of us."

To Sully's astonishment, Q threw back his head and laughed. It was a lovely sound; full, deep and genuine. Shaking his head, his own grin causing his cheeks to ache, Sully eased into traffic. It wasn't exactly driving off into the sunset. It was the middle of the day. And they weren't driving off into the wild blue yonder. They wouldn't be at their ranch for another two weeks, but as they headed for the hotel, Sully knew he'd finally found his happy ever after and despite all the changes in his life, he couldn't be happier.

The End

I do hope you enjoyed this short story about Sully and Q. Sully had a lot of growing up to do in this story and I was proud of how he turned out in the end. Q never said a lot, but then those staunch marines never do.

This isn't the end of the Alpha and Omega series. I have a delicious idea about an officious omega who has been tugging at my brain for months. I am certainly looking forward to telling his story when I have the time.

In the meantime, please watch for new books in the Gods Made Me Do It series, the Balance series, Arrowtown and so much more in the coming months. My writing to-do list never gets any shorter but I have so much fun sharing these stories with you.

If you did enjoy this story, please think about leaving a review. They mean the world to us authors and really help encourage sales to new readers. And don't forget, I love hearing from you. My contact details can be found in the "About the Author" section at the back of the book.

Hug the one you love.

Lisa.

Other Books By Lisa Oliver

Cloverleah Pack

Book 1 – The Reluctant Wolf – Kane and Shawn

Book 2 – The Runaway Cat – Griff and Diablo

Book 3 – When No Doesn't Cut It – Damien and Scott

Book 3.5 – Never Go Back – Scott and Damien's Trip and a free story about Malacai and Elijah

Book 4 – Calming the Enforcer – Troy and Anton

Book 5 – Getting Close to the Omega – Dean and Matthew

Book 6 – Fae for All – Jax, Aelfric and Fafnir (M/M/M)

Book 7 – Watching Out for Fangs – Josh and Vadim

Book 8 – Tangling with Bears – Tobias, Luke and Kurt (M/M/M)

Book 9 – Angel in Black Leather – Adair and Vassago

Book 9.5 – Scenes from Cloverleah – four short stories featuring the men we've come to love

Book 10 – On The Brink – Teilo, Raff and Nereus (M/M/M)

Book 11 – (as yet untitled) – Marius and (shush, it's a secret) (Coming soon)

The God's Made Me Do It
(Cloverleah spin off series)

Get Over It – Madison and Sebastian's story

You've Got to be Kidding – Poseidon and (another secret lol) (coming soon)

Bound and Bonded Series

Book One – Don't Touch – Levi and Steel

Book Two – Topping the Dom – Pearson and Dante

Book Three – Total Submission – Kyle and Teric

Book Four – Fighting Fangs – Ace and Devin

Book Five – No Mate of Mine – Roger and Cam

Book Six – Undesirable Mate – Phillip and Kellen

(Yes, there is a spin off series coming and all I can say about that, at this point, is soon, I'm sorry, but it hasn't been forgotten).

Stockton Wolves Series

Book One – Get off My Case – Shane and Dimitri

Book Two – Copping a Lot of Sin – Ben, Sin and Gabriel (M/M/M)

Book Three – Mace's Awakening – Mace and Roan

Book Four – Don't Bite – Trent and Alexi

Book Five – Tell Me the Truth – Captain Reynolds and Nico

Alpha and Omega Series

Book One – The Biker's Omega – Marly and Trent

Book Two – Dance Around the Cop – Zander and Terry

Book 2.5 – Change of Plans - Q and Sully (You just read it ☺)

Book Three – The Artist and His Alpha – Caden and Sean

Book Four – Harder in Heels – Ronan and Asaph

Book 4.5 – A Touch of Spring – Bronson and Harley

The Portrain Pack and Coven

The Power of the Bite – Dax and Zane

The Fangs Between Us – Broz and Van – a Portrain Coven and Pack Prequel (coming soon).

Balance – Angels and Demons

The Viper's Heart – Raziel and Botis

Passion Punched King – Anael and Zagan – (coming soon)

Arrowtown

A Tiger's Tale – Ra and Seth

Snake Snack – Simon and...you have to wait and see (coming soon)

Also under the penname Lee Oliver

Northern States Pack Series

Book One – Ranger's End Game – Ranger and Aiden

Book Two – Cam's Promise – Cam and his secret – (coming soon)

Shifter's Uprising Series – Lisa Oliver in conjunction with Thomas J. Oliver

Book One – Uncaged – Carlin and Lucas

Book Two – Fly Free (Coming soon)

[I have purposefully removed the dates my new releases may be due – there are two new series currently under development (the B&B spin off and a new dragon series) and of course a whole host of other books that will be written. But I have been having some personal mental health issues so I can't promise **when** new titles will be arriving. All I can promise is that I am still writing and new books will be released as soon as possible. I am sorry for any inconvenience.]

About the Author

Lisa Oliver had been writing non-fiction books for years when visions of half dressed, buff men started invading her dreams. Unable to resist the lure of her stories, Lisa decided to switch to fiction books, and now stories about her men clamor to get out from under her fingertips.

When Lisa is not writing, she is usually reading with a cup of tea always at hand. Her grown children and grandchildren sometimes try and pry her away from the computer and have found that the best way to do it is to promise her chocolate. Lisa will do anything for chocolate.

Lisa loves to hear from her readers and other writers. You can friend her on Facebook (http://www.facebook.com/lisaoliverauthor), catch up on what's happening at her blog

(http://www.supernaturalsmut.com)
or email her directly at
yoursintuitively@gmail.com.

(I also now have a new group on
Facebook: Lisa's Wolfpack -
https://www.facebook.com/groups/2
17413318738434/.)

Printed in Great Britain
by Amazon

36752835R00106